# EXTRAORDINARY

# EXTRAORDINARY

Miriam Spitzer Franklin

Sky Pony Press
New York

Sky Pony Press books may be purchased in bulk at special discounts for sales promotion, corporate gifts, fund-raising, or educational purposes. Special editions can also be created to specifications. For details, contact the Special Sales Department, Sky Pony Press, 307 West 36th Street, 11th Floor, New York, NY 10018 or info@skyhorsepublishing.com.

Sky Pony® is a registered trademark of Skyhorse Publishing, Inc.®, a Delaware corporation.

Visit our website at www.skyponypress.com.

10 9 8 7 6 5 4 3 2 1

Library of Congress Cataloging-in-Publication Data

Franklin, Miriam Spitzer.
Extraordinary / Miriam Spitzer Franklin.
pages cm
Summary: Pansy often backed out of things her best friend, Anna, wanted to do, including attending the sleepaway camp where Anna contracted meningitis and became disabled, but when Pansy learns that surgery might restore Anna to her old self, she will do anything to become extraordinary in time for Anna's return.
ISBN 978-1-63220-402-8 (hardback) -- ISBN 978-1-63220-822-4 (ebook)
[1. Best friends--Fiction. 2. Friendship--Fiction. 3. People with disabilities--Fiction. 4. Self-actualization (Psychology)--Fiction.] I. Title.
PZ7.1.F754Ext 2015
[Fic]--dc23
2014042500

Cover design and illustration by Brian Peterson

Printed in the United States of America

*For my dad*

## CHAPTER ONE

# Fourteen Weeks, Four Days

It was the first day of fifth grade, and I had a promise to keep. Ever since spring break, I'd woken up with an ache inside of me, like I'd been swallowing rocks all night. But today, I felt a hundred times lighter. Instead of rocks in my stomach, today I felt the fluttering of butterfly wings.

I glanced down at my necklace—the one with half a heart and the words BEST FRIENDS written across it. I jumped out of bed and grabbed the scissors on my dresser. Most people would think I was nuts, but I knew what I had to do. I gathered up my hair in a ponytail, opened up the scissors, and began to cut.

My hair didn't fall to the ground with one snip the way Anna's had at Shear Magic Salon back in March. I felt like

I was sawing through my stack of *American Girl* magazines, but I kept on cutting. Finally, my ponytail dropped from my hand and fell to the floor with a *thump*.

I stared down at the pile of hair. I closed my eyes, then opened them again. The ponytail was still on the floor.

My eyes traveled up to the mirror. My long hair was gone. Staring back at me was a girl with much shorter hair, bigger eyes, and a longer neck. I looked different, and I knew that inside I'd become a different person, too.

I turned away from the mirror and pulled out my special box from my bottom dresser drawer. I had covered the box in pink construction paper, decorated it with hearts, and written the word ANNA on it with glitter markers.

I picked up a photo taken a few weeks before Anna went to camp last spring without me, right after we promised each other we'd cut our hair for Locks of Love. Short-haired Anna peered back at me, her eyes shining as a big smile stretched across her face. We were outside Shear Magic Salon, and Anna had her arm around my shoulder, hidden under the long hair that fell halfway down my back.

I flipped through the other photos. Anna and I dressed up as salt and pepper shakers for Halloween. Hanging upside down from the jungle gym. Holding onto the same boogie board as the waves crash around us. I lingered on my favorite—from last summer on the Fourth of July. We wore red, white, and blue hats with sparkly tassels sticking out of the top, and we had our arms around each other, making silly faces.

Pulling my eyes away from the photos, I stared into the mirror, thinking about how I could magically transform into the kind of person I wanted to be. This year I had to become all the things I'd never been before: Brave. Daring. Smart. Talented. Extraordinary in every way, like Anna.

I had to become extraordinary because, yesterday, I heard the most amazing news. Anna was going to have surgery in a few months that could fix her brain and turn her back into the person I used to know. And when she woke up in the hospital and saw me again for the first time, I was going to be the best friend she could ever have.

If I turned into an extraordinary person, then Anna had to forgive me for all the promises I'd broken. And she'd have to forget about the huge fight we had right before she went to sleep-away camp over spring break—the fight that ended when Anna asked me to leave and slammed the door behind me.

The next time I saw her was in the hospital. Anna couldn't talk, she couldn't understand what people were saying, and she didn't act like she knew me at all. And if she remembered the fight, I sure couldn't tell.

"Pansy! Time for breakfast!" Mom called. I shook the memory of Hospital Anna right out of my head and ran down the stairs, two at a time.

"Hi, Mom, Dad," I said, dropping into a chair at the kitchen table.

"Hi, honey. What do you want for . . ." Mom's voice trailed off as she looked up from the lunch she was packing. Her mouth dropped open and her eyes got big and round. "Pansy Louisa Smith! What in the world have you done with your hair?"

Dad peered at me from over his newspaper. Then he choked on his toast.

I ran my fingers down my neck, which felt pretty good without all that heavy hair against it. "I'm giving it to Locks of Love. To help girls who lost their hair from cancer."

Silence. Dad wiped crumbs from his mouth and cleared his throat. Mom was still staring at me like I'd dyed my hair in rainbow colors and gotten a Mohawk. But all I did was cut off my ponytail!

I poured myself a glass of orange juice. "Remember when I was going to cut my hair back in March?"

"Of course, honey," Mom said, her voice softening. "You and Anna planned it together."

"Well, I finally did it," I said. "I promised Anna I'd do it, and it's not nice to break a promise."

Mom nodded, then popped a bagel in the toaster. She and Dad gave each other The Look, which they'd been giving each other a lot this summer. It meant, "I'm worried about Pansy. Maybe she needs to talk to a psychiatrist."

Mom had asked more than once if I wanted to see a doctor "to talk about things." I'd told her no—that I was definitely not interested in talking to some stranger. I hadn't convinced them, though. They didn't think I could hear them from across the hall, but it wasn't so hard to figure out they were talking about me in hushed voices in their room at night.

While the bagel was toasting, Mom smoothed my hair with her hand and gave me a hug. "Are you all right?"

"I'm great. It's the first day of fifth grade. And I've always wanted to give my hair to Locks of Love, so I thought today would be a good day for it."

"But why didn't you tell me?" Mom set the bagel on the table. "I would have taken you to the salon. There are people who cut hair for a living, you know."

I tucked a loose strand behind my ear. "I like my hair the way it is. Well, except it makes my neck look funny. Do you think my neck is too long?"

Dad laughed.

"You have a lovely neck," Mom said with a smile. Then she picked up her phone and checked her schedule like she did every day. "I have to show a couple of houses this morning, but I'm free all afternoon. I'll call my hairdresser and see if she can fit you in after school."

What was the hairdresser going to do—glue my hair back on my head? "Mommm . . . I already told you, I think it looks perfect."

"Ellen, why don't we talk about this later?" Dad said to Mom. "It takes guts to be a true individual."

"Thanks," I said. I sat up a little straighter in my seat. *A true individual.* That's what I needed if I was on my way to being extraordinary.

Dad winked at me. Mom sighed and set her phone down.

"So, we were thinking," Dad said, glancing at the clock. "Do you want me to give you a ride on your first day?"

"A ride?" I looked up from my bagel. "To school?"

"Sure," Dad said, but he looked away, busying himself with folding up the newspaper. "Since it's your first day of fifth grade and all."

*Oh.* The first day of a new school year *without Anna* is what he meant. The old Pansy would have taken him up on it. Instead, I said, "I told Andy I'm meeting him, like always."

"Oh, okay," Dad said. "We were just wondering—"

"No, I mean, yeah, I'm fine." I glanced up at the clock. Cutting off my hair had taken longer than I thought. I gulped down the last of my breakfast and ran to the shoe basket next to the door.

I strained my ears to hear my parents' conversation as I slipped on my shoes but couldn't make out their words. I was sure they were talking about me.

"Bye, Mom! Bye, Dad!" I grabbed my backpack and headed out the door. Luckily, Greenview Elementary was only a few blocks away. I took off in a run, hoping Andy, Anna's twin brother, hadn't left without me.

I spotted him as I rounded the corner. He was waiting on his front porch, glancing at his watch as he paced back and forth.

"Hey!" I stopped to catch my breath. "Sorry I'm late."

Mrs. Liddell stuck her head out the door. "Hi, Pansy!"

"Hi, Mrs. Liddell. How's Anna doing today?"

Mrs. Liddell smiled. "Great. She's already had a big breakfast, and she has a therapy appointment this morning . . . Oh, wow, I love your new haircut!"

"Thanks. I cut it this morning."

"This morning?" Her eyes opened wide. "You did it yourself?"

"Mom, we gotta go," Andy said. Mrs. Liddell gave Andy a hug, and he squirmed away as fast as he could. "Come on, Pansy," he said, hopping off the porch.

"Have a great day!" Mrs. Liddell called to us.

When we got to the end of the driveway, I ran my hand over my short hair and smiled at Andy. "So, what do you think? Do you like it?"

He stared at me for a minute. Then he shook his head. "No. You look weird."

I rolled my eyes and started walking again, faster this time. "You're just like my mom. She tried to make me an appointment this afternoon with her hairdresser."

"It's not that," Andy said. "I don't get why you'd cut it off, that's all."

"For Locks of Love!" I said. "You know, like Anna did."

Andy sucked in his breath and looked away from me. I wanted to explain why I *had* to cut my hair—that I'd overheard my mom talking to his mom on the phone and that I knew all about Anna's brain surgery. I wanted to tell him about my plans to become extraordinary so Anna would forgive me. But the words got stuck in my throat.

We walked the rest of the way in silence.

"I hope we don't have a lot of homework this year," Andy finally said as we neared the front doors. "I hope Miss Quetzel's not as bad as some of the other fifth-grade teachers. Last year, I heard that Mrs. Sandora assigned a five-page paper for homework on the very first day of school."

I raised an eyebrow at him. "Five pages? On the first night? I bet someone made that up to scare you."

"It's true. Jacob Lambuca had her last year. Everyone had to write about how they spent their summer vacation."

"I don't believe it." I shook my head, wondering how I'd fill up five pages about my vacation. *Pushed Anna on the swing. Handed Anna a toy. Talked to Anna even though she didn't understand what I was saying. Played with Andy in his treehouse. Went home and thought about Anna.* "Besides, Miss Quetzel's a new teacher. She's probably much nicer than Mrs. Sandora."

"Maybe. Hey, Pansy?"

"What?"

"Why are you wearing two different colored shoes?"

I stopped in front of the school and looked down at my feet. One pink sneaker . . . and one blue!

*Uh-oh.*

My stomach dropped to my toes. Would people be like Dad and think that I was "a true individual"? Or would they think I was plain weird?

Anna would have laughed, and then she would have offered to switch one of her shoes so it would be like we'd mixed everything up on purpose.

Andy just shrugged and pushed open the doors without saying another word.

Miss Quetzel stood in the doorway of Room 5A. Her red hair fell past her shoulders in bouncy ringlets, and her green eyes sparkled as she smiled at me. I could already tell she was a lot nicer than old Mrs. Sandora.

"Welcome to fifth grade!" she greeted us. "Look for your nametag, and then you can start on some fun activity sheets that are on your desk."

I smiled back and walked into the room. Maybe if I pretended I didn't notice my shoes, no one else would, either. As I wandered around looking for my nametag, a punch landed smack on my shoulder.

I turned to find Zach Turansky, the most obnoxious boy in the fifth grade, standing behind me. Just my luck. He pointed at my lopsided haircut, an ugly grin on his face.

"What happened to you—did your head get caught in a lawnmower?"

A couple boys laughed. My cheeks blazed. What I really wanted to do was punch him right back. Not just because he deserved it, but because of the mean and rotten things he'd said to Andy last year.

Instead, I took a deep breath and looked Zach straight in the eye. "I cut my hair for Locks of Love," I said, courage soaring through me. "Not that it's any of your business." Then I turned away from him, holding my head high.

Even though Zach and the boys were still making cracks about me, I felt a smile curve up my face as I walked away from them. I'd stood up to Zach, when it used to be Anna who always had a good comeback ready. Even with a lopsided haircut and mismatched shoes, I could do this. I could become extraordinary for Anna, and when she came out of surgery, we'd become best friends again, the way it was supposed to be.

## CHAPTER TWO

# Fourteen Weeks, Four Days

I made my way to the front row, where Andy was pointing to the desk next to his. My name was printed neatly on the nametag. Andy gave me a thumbs-up as I slid into my chair. A few minutes later, Miss Quetzel asked us to put away our activity sheets as she passed out a piece of paper with the words CLASS DISCIPLINE POLICY written at the top.

By the time you make it to the last year of elementary school, you pretty much know everything that might show up on such a handout. So it didn't take long for my mind to wander.

School would be a lot more interesting with some new rules. What if you had to yell out, "Warty pickles!" whenever you had to use the pencil sharpener? Or what if one of the class jobs was being the cheerleader? Every time someone answered correctly, the cheerleader would have to clap, cheer, or turn a cartwheel.

I was so busy thinking up new rules that I missed something Miss Quetzel said. It must have been good because the quiet room suddenly bubbled over with excitement.

Miss Quetzel clapped her hands together. When everyone settled down, she said, "Class, I know that everyone will have a great time at the Good Citizens party in December. But here's the catch." She paused dramatically and looked at all of us. "You will have to *earn* the party *as a class.* There will be opportunities to earn points for good behavior, but points will also be taken away for disruptive and disrespectful behavior. Therefore, it is very important that we work together and remind each other to behave like Good Citizens throughout the day. And here's something I'll bet you don't know about me: I've been a figure skater most of my life. So anyone who wants skating lessons, I'll be glad to help. Plus, I'll reserve the party room at the Ice Palace, so we can have a real celebration with popcorn, cake, and soda!"

Everyone erupted into cheers again. Everyone, that is, except me. The Good Citizens party would take place *at the ice-skating rink*? Why couldn't Miss Quetzel be a champion bowler or cake-baker instead? Of all the places for a fun party, the Ice Palace was at the bottom of my list.

Last winter, Anna convinced me to sign up for skating lessons. She had glided off right away, while I spent most of the time sitting on the ice. My toes froze, my ankles blistered, and my nose ran for the whole hour. The best part of the afternoon—actually, the *only* good part—was when I finally pulled off my skates and headed to the warming area for a cup of hot chocolate.

"I quit," I had told Anna afterward. "I don't have to do something more than once to know I hate it." And I had meant it. At the time, anyway.

But . . . this was my chance to make it up to Anna. I needed to show her I was the type of person who followed through on promises even when it was tough. If Anna's surgery was at the beginning of December, she could be totally cured in time for the Good Citizens party. Anna would know I'd changed when I put on my skates and glided along beside her.

I thought about the Good Citizens party for the rest of the morning. I pointed my toes underneath my desk, imagining I was one of those beautiful figure skaters I liked to watch on TV. Now I just had to convince my parents to sign me up for lessons, which wasn't going to be easy since I'd quit the last time.

By lunchtime, I decided that Miss Quetzel was the most awesome teacher I'd ever had. I thought she liked me, too. She'd called me by name, smiled at me, and put her hand on my shoulder when she walked past my desk.

"Miss Quetzel is cool," I said to Andy as we sat down in the cafeteria. Miss Quetzel had told us to fill in the seats at the long table, so we ended up next to Madison Poplin and a group of her friends. Madison was one of those popular girls that Anna and I never paid much attention to.

Andy opened his lunchbox and pulled out a baggie full of sliced Pop-Tarts. He never ate sandwiches. "Do you think Miss Quetzel can really figure skate?" he asked me.

"Of course she can. Do you think she'd make it up?"

Andy pushed his glasses up on his nose. "I wonder how good she is, that's all."

"You might find out at the end of the semester," Madison said, joining our conversation, "if the class makes it."

I pushed my shoulders back and sat up tall. "I know we will," I told her. "I can't wait!"

"Do you know how to ice-skate?" Madison asked me.

"Sure." I cleared my throat and looked over at Andy. He knew all about how I had quit skating lessons last year. "I mean, I can skate a little."

Madison shrugged, then looked down at my feet. "Do you know you're wearing two different shoes?"

For a moment, I froze. The morning had gone so well I'd forgotten about my mismatched shoes. But now the other girls nearby were peering under the table. Hannah let out a big giggle. At least Emma put a hand over her mouth like she was trying to be polite.

I looked down at my feet, then glanced under the table at Madison's. Wouldn't you know? She wore white sandals with sunflowers on them, which not only matched each other but also matched her outfit.

"Well . . ." I stalled, trying to come up with a good answer. Madison Poplin was not the kind of person to wear mismatched shoes. Actually, she wasn't the kind of person to wear mismatched *anything*. For example, today she wore a long pink shirt with big yellow flowers all over it, pink leggings, a headband that matched her shirt, and sunflower earrings.

Madison was the kind of girl who competed in pageants. Last year, she'd won the Junior Miss title. I'd seen the picture of her on the front page of the paper. She looked like a princess as she rode in a parade float, a silver crown sitting on top of her head.

I chewed on the inside of my cheek, still trying to think of what to say to her. I was never into princesses, not even when I was little. Anna and I went through a stage where we both pretended to be fairies, and we wore princessy gowns with wings. Fairies were a lot more exciting, because at least they could fly and get into all kinds of adventures instead of just sitting there like princesses, looking pretty.

"I mean," Madison continued when I didn't answer her, "are you wearing two different shoes because you couldn't find the other one of each pair and luckily you ended up with a right and a left, or did you get dressed in the dark and you didn't realize your shoes didn't match?"

"No." I took a deep breath. And then I thought about what Anna would say if she were the one wearing shoes that didn't match. "I'm wearing two different colored shoes because when I woke up this morning I decided I'd like to wear a blue shoe and a pink shoe. And that's what I did."

"Oh." Madison took a bite out of her sandwich, chewing carefully. Finally she swallowed. "My mother would never let me wear mismatched shoes to school."

"I don't think my mother noticed," I told her. Which was the truth. If I'd planned it on purpose, Mom wouldn't have liked it, just like she didn't want me to go to school with a lopsided haircut. But she probably wouldn't have stopped me. And Dad would have laughed and said I was "expressing my individuality."

Madison studied me some more. "I like your haircut."

"Thanks," I said, staring at her golden hair that shimmered as it tumbled down her back. "I cut it myself."

"I can tell," Madison said.

"Me too," Hannah said. "It's really crooked."

I shot Hannah a dirty look. I wanted to yell, "Who cares if I don't look like a fashion model? If you don't like the way I look, then go sit somewhere else!"

But I figured yelling at people, especially popular ones, was not the best way to start fifth grade. Before anyone could say anything else about my hair or shoes, Madison turned to Andy.

"So, how's Anna?"

Andy became very interested in his Pop-Tart. "She's okay," he said so quietly I could barely hear him.

Someone had blown up a balloon inside of me and it pushed up against my stomach. I bit my tongue to keep from blurting out, "Anna's having brain surgery, and she'll be cured in December!"

"Guess what?" I said instead. "Anna jumped off the diving board this summer."

"Really?" Madison said. "Can she still swim?"

"Of course. You can't keep Anna away from the water," I said, thinking about the blue swim team ribbons covering her bulletin board. I didn't tell them she had to wear a swim vest so she wouldn't sink.

"Did someone have to take her up on the diving board?" Emma asked.

"I guess. But she jumps off without a problem." I laughed. "She's still a better swimmer than I am."

"If it were my mom, she'd never let Anna go in a swimming pool," Hannah said. "It's too dangerous. What if she drowns?"

"She wears a vest," Andy said. "Mom wouldn't let her do anything that's not safe."

"But still . . ." Hannah said.

"Hannah," Madison said impatiently. "I'm sure Anna still remembers how."

"She remembers a lot of things," I said. "Her brain just needs time to heal."

"Will she ever be able to come back to school?" Hannah asked.

"She's going to a new school now," Andy said. He was talking about Camden Academy, a place kids went to if they couldn't go to a regular school.

"I bet she'll come back to our school someday soon," I said, glancing at Andy. He shifted his eyes back to his lunch.

Emma smiled. "It would be great to have Anna in our class again."

Andy shrugged and popped the last of the Pop-Tart in his mouth. "So," he said, "do you think Miss Quetzel can land a triple jump?"

Silence fell over the table. It was odd the way Andy had changed the subject when we were talking about Anna. I tried to catch his eye, but he wouldn't look at me.

"I'm sure Miss Quetzel's telling the truth," I finally said. "Why would she lie to us about being a figure skater?"

"I wonder if she can do a back flip," Andy said. "Mom took me to this show where the skaters did back flips. Do you know what might happen if you missed your landing on that trick?"

"I've never seen anyone fall on a back flip," I said.

"It could happen. You could fly through the air, sprawled out, and land SPLAT! Just like an egg cracked open on the sidewalk."

"A person does not crack open like an egg!" I said. "Besides, we're talking about falling on the ice, not the sidewalk."

"Even worse," Andy said. "First, your insides would ooze out all over the ice. Then they'd freeze and stick to the surface."

"Gross!" I yelled. Soon everyone at the table was giggling, even Madison. Andy could always get people to laugh, especially Anna. And in a few months, she'd be sitting there next to me, right where she belonged, laughing, too.

***

At dinner that night, I told my parents all about my day. Then I asked the big question: "Can I take ice-skating lessons?"

Mom frowned. "Am I hearing things, or did my daughter just ask for ice-skating lessons?"

"You heard right, Mom." I speared a green bean with my fork. "Miss Quetzel's a figure skater, and she's taking all of us to the Ice Palace if we earn the Good Citizens party at the end of the semester. So I have until Christmas to get into shape."

"You think you might land some double axels by then?" Dad teased.

"Daaad . . ."

Mom shook her head. "Pansy, I'm glad you want to give it another try. Although if I remember correctly, your exact words were, 'I'd rather wrestle a hairy tarantula than ice-skate again.'"

I shuddered. "I never said that. I'd never touch a tarantula, not in a million trillion years!"

"That's exactly my point," Mom said. "We can't afford to throw out money on lessons for something you don't enjoy. How do I know you won't quit after one lesson like you did last time? The rink refused to give us a refund, remember?"

I nodded. I'd heard all about it for weeks. "I need a second chance," I said. "I promise, I won't quit this time."

"Ice-skating's not for everyone, Pansy," Dad said. "Take me, for example. You won't catch me putting on skates."

I groaned. They didn't get it at all. And, of course, I couldn't tell them the real reason I just *had* to take ice-skating lessons. They wouldn't understand my plan to try to become extraordinary.

Mom and Dad looked at each other. I guess they were doing that silent-communication thing because Mom finally said, "I'll tell you what. Why don't you dust the cobwebs off that pair of roller blades we bought you for Christmas last year? Start practicing on those skates, and if you stick with it for a while, then we'll enroll you in lessons."

I thought about it for a minute. I could practice without other people watching, and I wouldn't have to worry about frozen fingers and toes. I could prove to my parents that I was serious, and there would still be time for real lessons before the party.

"Okay. I'll practice every day, you'll see."

"That's my girl," Dad said with a grin.

## CHAPTER THREE

# Fourteen Weeks

Today, we're going to work on setting goals for the grading period," Miss Quetzel announced on Friday morning. "I bet you can do anything you set your mind to. So, I'd like for you to write down three goals and include the steps you'll take to reach your goals."

Miss Quetzel wrote an example on the board:

MY GOALS:

1. To make A/B Honor Roll—I will do my home-work, study for tests, and try my best.

2.

3.

After Miss Quetzel went over her example, we were on our own. While other kids gazed at their blank papers or copied the example from the board, I wrote in my neatest handwriting: My goal: to be extraordinary in every way.

But what did that mean, exactly? It made me think of a picture in *A Child's Book of Poetry*. A girl sat in a rowboat in the sky, trying to catch stars in her net.

How would I ever catch one of those stars?

As the minutes on the clock ticked away, I wrote:

1. MAKE A'S ON ALL OF MY TESTS.
2. BECOME MISS QUETZEL'S FAVORITE STUDENT.
3. BE FEARLESS.
4. BECOME A GOOD ICE-SKATER. PRACTICE ROLLER-BLADING EVERY DAY SO I CAN SKATE WITH ANNA AT THE PARTY.
5. JOIN GIRL SCOUTS. THIS TIME, LEARN TO GO CAMP- ING IN THE WOODS EVEN IF THERE  ARE GROSS BUGS IN THE BATHROOMS.
6. DON'T BREAK MY PROMISES.

I sat back and read over my list. I chewed my pencil and thought some more. Finally, I added one that didn't have anything to do with being extraordinary. But it's something I'd started by accident, and I'd been doing it all week, even though I couldn't explain why:

7. WEAR MISMATCHED SHOES EVERY DAY.

Miss Quetzel's voice broke through my thoughts. "Okay, everyone. Please pass your papers to the front. I'll keep your goals on file, and at the end of the grading period we'll take them out and see what you've accomplished."

The smile slipped off my face. There was no way I was passing that paper to the front with the others. I'd only listed one main goal instead of three. I'd written about stuff that didn't have anything to do with school. And even worse, letting my teacher know I was trying to become her favorite student could only backfire. So I snapped my notebook shut and stared straight ahead, hoping she wouldn't notice.

"If you didn't finish writing your goals, you'll need to do it for homework," Miss Quetzel said with a knowing look in my direction. "Now, let's get started with our speed drills for the day."

Some kids groaned. I was one of them. Then I remembered my goal about trying to be Miss Quetzel's favorite student, so I tried to act like Madison Poplin, who was clearing her desk with a smile on her face.

Miss Quetzel had started the drills earlier that week, telling us it was important to review basic skills. When I'd written down that I planned to make A's on all my tests, I'd completely forgotten about speed drills. My brain is just not wired to think fast, which means I'll be stuck on twos for the rest of my life.

Miss Quetzel placed a sheet of paper facedown on my desk. "Is everyone ready? All right, three, two, one, you may begin!"

After a mad shuffle of papers, the sounds of pencils scratching filled the room. I turned my quiz over and it floated off my desk onto the floor. I reached over to pick it up and dropped my pencil.

*Tick, tick.* An imaginary clock ticked in my head, counting down the seconds. The pounding of my heart echoed in my ears. I scrambled for my pencil, slammed my paper down on the desk, and raced through the multiplication facts as fast as I could.

*Ding.*

"Time's up!" Miss Quetzel called out way too cheerily. "Put your pencils down, and pass your papers to the front."

I stared down at my multiplication quiz. Four problems left. One fewer than the day before. Miss Quetzel flipped through the papers. "It looks like quite a few of you will be moving up to sixes on Monday," she said with a smile.

\*\*\*

"I can't believe some people are still on the twos," Hannah said at lunch a little while later. All week long we'd ended up sitting near Madison and her friends in the cafeteria, since they all brought lunch from home, too. "I learned to count by twos in kindergarten!"

"Not everyone is good at math," said Madison. I was sure she was one of those people moving on to the sixes on Monday.

"You don't have to be good at math to do speed drills," Hannah said. "All you have to do is memorize. Anyone can do that, especially by fifth grade."

I felt my cheeks heat up. I wanted to dump my macaroni and cheese right in Hannah's lap. Instead, I turned to Andy. "Did you see that special on the Discovery Channel last night? The one about the baby animals?"

"What special?" Andy asked. "The only thing on Discovery Channel last night was *Saving Planet Earth*."

"Well, you must have been on the wrong channel, then." I squirmed in my seat. Hannah and Madison were still watching me, listening in on my conversation. So I tried to make it exciting. "It was all about animals that are carried around on their moms' backs, like opossums and sloths and manatees."

"Manatees? They are way too slippery. How could they carry babies on their backs?"

"Well, they just do, that's all. The babies hold on with their tiny toenails."

"Baby manatees do not have toenails!" Andy yelled out, and his voice was loud enough that the whole row of girls started giggling.

"They do so. You should have watched it."

"I couldn't watch it, Pansy. I told you that *Saving Planet Earth* was on the Discovery Channel."

"Maybe it was another channel, then. Forget it, okay?" I tried to give Andy my best just-drop-it look. I should have known better than to try and make up a TV special about animals. Andy was an expert on those kinds of things. And why were the girls so interested in our conversation anyway? When were they going to start their own conversation, like they usually did?

Andy didn't give up, though. "What channel? I really want to know so I can write and tell them what my friend saw even though it's impossible—"

The girls giggled again.

I kicked Andy under the table, hoping he'd look up so I could send him the message I was done talking about manatees. I'd only brought it up to keep the girls from talking about speed drills. At least I'd accomplished *something.*

Andy still didn't get the message. "OUCH!" he yelled. "What'd you kick me for?"

The girls burst into laughter.

*** 

"Thanks a lot," I said to him when we headed back to the classroom after lunch.

Andy gave me a blank look. "For what?"

I stopped right in the middle of the hall. "You know *exactly* what I'm talking about."

Andy shook his head. "No, I don't. What are you so mad about?"

"Pansy! Andy!" Miss Quetzel called from the back of the line. "Keep moving. And no talking in the hall."

I turned away from him, walking ahead quickly.

Once back in the classroom, Miss Quetzel turned off the lights for a movie about the Declaration of Independence.

"Remember to take good notes," she said. "There may be a quiz afterward."

"Can I borrow a piece of paper?" Andy asked me even though he had a full notebook.

I tore a sheet from my notebook and shoved it over to his desk without looking at him.

I was trying my best to write down facts when Andy slipped a folded piece of paper onto my desk. I opened it up: I KNOW YOU'RE ANGRY AT ME. IS IT BECAUSE I CAUGHT YOU IN A LIE AT LUNCH?

I heaved a humongous sigh in Andy's direction. *Well, if he's so dense, I may as well spell it out for him.* "It has nothing to do with lying. You were trying to make me look stupid in front of all those girls," I spat back at him.

Andy scrawled something on another piece of paper and tossed it to me. WHO CARES WHAT A BUNCH OF DUMB GIRLS THINK?

I rolled my eyes. *I care.* But I didn't want to tell him that. I turned my attention back to the movie. A few minutes later, another folded piece of paper came across my desk. I think George Washington bought his hair at Wigs R Us was written in Andy's sloppy handwriting.

I held back a grin, shoving the note back onto his desk. I wasn't about to forgive him so easily. But as hard as I tried to pay attention, I kept staring at the wigs of all the founding fathers instead. Didn't they know how stupid they looked?

A few minutes later, another piece of paper landed on my desk. This time I had to work harder to keep in my giggles as I read, I think Thomas Jefferson is going to try out for the ballet. Do you like his tights?

I didn't answer the notes, but they kept right on coming. I shoved each one back across Andy's desk. But he didn't stop. The jokes got worse and worse. When Andy drew a picture of the founding fathers wearing ballet tutus and big curly wigs, the laughter exploded right out of my mouth.

Andy started laughing, too, and there was nothing either of us could do to stop.

"Andy Liddell! Pansy Smith!" Miss Quetzel shot a warning in our direction.

I clamped a hand over my mouth. I inhaled the laugh, and it came out as a snort. Andy's whole body shook as he tried to keep the laughter from escaping.

I'd gone over the edge of the waterfall as far as the giggles went. There was no turning back, and there was nothing anyone could do to stop it.

Miss Quetzel erased a point from the Good Citizens chart and then stepped in front of my desk. "What's with you two today? I think you'd better excuse yourselves if you can't pull it together. I know you don't want to spend any more than ten minutes of your recess in detention hall," she said sharply.

I clamped a hand over my mouth and scooted out of the room, ignoring the dirty looks of some of my classmates.

"Thanks a lot, Pansy," Hannah whispered as I rushed past her desk. But I was too busy giggling to pay much attention to her.

Andy and I collapsed against the wall by the water fountain, trying to catch our breaths.

"Pansy?" Andy asked a few minutes later, after we had calmed down. "Not mad at me anymore, are you?"

I shook my head. "Only for getting me in trouble."

"Don't worry," Andy said with a grin. "I got myself in trouble, too."

It wasn't until we were back in the classroom taking our quiz that it all sunk in: I was missing part of recess *and* I'd caused the class to lose a Good Citizens point.

I tugged on my hair. There were also those goals I'd made about being Miss Quetzel's favorite student and making straight A's. This was not the way to go about it. Perfect students did not have total giggle fits during social studies movies.

To make things worse, I flunked the quiz. At least I wasn't alone in that—Andy held a paper with a red F and the words PAY ATTENTION! written on the top.

I shoved the quiz in my desk, burying it beneath a pile of books. I hoped Miss Quetzel would forget all about it, just like I planned to do.

I glanced over at Andy, who was crumpling up his quiz and shoving it in his desk also. That's when I felt a smile slowly spread across my face. If Anna had seen Andy's drawings, she would have giggled along with us. I had three whole months to reach my goals, and I wasn't about to let one giggle fit and an F on a quiz slow me down.

## CHAPTER FOUR

# Thirteen Weeks, Six Days

How's the skating coming?" Dad asked on Saturday morning as he sat down next to me on the sofa.

"Skating?" I nibbled on a piece of toast with butter. I didn't turn toward my dad, staring at the cartoon on the TV instead.

Dad pulled off his gardening gloves. Then he flicked off the TV.

"Daaaad! I was watching that!"

Dad ignored me. "You *are* the girl who was begging for ice-skating lessons a few days ago, right?"

"Yeah, but—"

"You better get a move on, then. I saw the Liddells outside, and they said they're going to Gateway Park. It's a great day for roller-blading."

I popped the rest of the toast in my mouth and brushed off the crumbs on my pajamas. "I bet they've already left by now," I said hopefully.

"As a matter of fact, they're stopping by in fifteen minutes. Andy's bringing his skates."

"Great," I mumbled. Why would anyone want to ruin a perfect day by going roller-blading? I knew Andy hadn't come up with the idea on his own. He'd much rather spend the day reading mysteries in his tree house, drawing comic strips, or building with his new LEGO set.

Dad clapped me on the shoulder, picked up his gardening gloves, and headed back outside.

I guess that was his way of saying, "Good luck. You'll need it."

There went my nice lazy morning. I let out a big sigh. All week long I'd tried to be extraordinary, talking to people I didn't know and raising my hand in class even when I didn't know the answer. It was a lot of hard work, and I was ready for a day off. But there was no way out of this one, so I got dressed and waited on the front porch for the Liddells.

When I saw Mrs. Liddell, Andy, and Anna appear around the corner, my heart skipped a beat. Mrs. Liddell was pushing Anna in a wheelchair. She could have walked to the park. But it would take a really long time because she liked to wander around instead of going in the right direction.

I waved as I hopped off the steps to greet them. "Hi, Mrs. Liddell. Hey, Andy."

I squeezed Anna's hand, the one that wasn't clutching a pink teddy bear. "Hi, Anna! We're going skating today!"

Anna looked up at me with her big blue eyes. A crooked smile stretched across her face.

"Wish you could skate with us," I whispered so no one else could hear.

My dad had been right about one thing: it was a great day to be outside. Andy and I walked along behind Mrs. Liddell and Anna, talking about Saturday morning TV cartoons. White clouds dotted the blue sky. A breeze fluttered the leaves on the trees, which were beginning to change colors.

I picked up a yellow leaf and ran my fingers across it, feeling that butterfly flutter inside me again. Summer was turning to fall, and fall would turn into winter, like it did every year. And just like I knew the seasons would change, I knew that a bigger change would take place in a few months.

After Anna's stroke, the doctors said she'd never walk again. But only a couple months later, she started walking and even running. The doctors said that Anna had permanent brain damage and there wasn't a cure. But I knew the surgery would fix her brain, and soon she'd be roller-skating in the park with me, instead of sitting in a wheelchair, watching.

"I thought you gave up roller-blading," Andy said a little while later as we sat on the grass, lacing up our boots.

"That was last year," I told him. "I thought I'd give it another try."

Most people who'd seen me up on skates would have laughed and said I had the right idea last year when I quit. But not Andy. He just held out a hand to help me to my feet.

"We'll be at the playground," Mrs. Liddell said.

Andy nodded and began to make his way toward the paved path.

I hobbled on my wobbly skates over to Anna's wheelchair, which Mrs. Liddell had parked by a bench. "Just watch!" I told her. "I'm going to be a real pro!"

Anna looked into my eyes as though she understood what I'd said. She couldn't talk, of course, and if you told her to do something, she wouldn't. But when I spoke to her, I got the feeling she was really listening. I touched her golden half-heart necklace. And I wondered, as I did every time I saw her wear it, if Anna was still wearing that necklace when she came home from camp, after our big fight. Or had Mrs. Liddell dug it out of her jewelry box because she remembered how Anna *used* to wear it every day?

It was one of those questions I was dying to know the answer to, but I never had the guts to ask.

I touched the necklace I wore, the other half of the heart. As I stared into Anna's eyes, I could almost hear her say, "You can do it, Pansy!" Then she smiled out of one side of her mouth.

I smiled back. Anna believed in me. She always had.

I began walking on the grass toward the path where Andy waited. *I will not fall,* I told myself as I picked up one foot at a time. I felt a lot like a baby trying to walk across the living room rug for the first time. But I filled my head with positive thoughts.

If Anna believed in me, anything was possible.

*** 

I stepped onto the path and noticed the ducks for the first time. They floated across the lake, some of them dipping their heads beneath the surface for food, some quacking, some honking.

All my good thoughts disappeared. *Poof!* Learning to roller-blade on a path that surrounded a big lake suddenly seemed like a really terrible idea.

Andy didn't seem to be bothered by the large amount of water we could suddenly find ourselves submerged in. He pushed off unsteadily, arms flailing for balance. "Let's go!" he yelled as he took off with awkward strokes.

*Okay. Take a deep breath,* I told myself. *Just. Don't. Look. At. The. Water.*

I concentrated on my feet and the path ahead. The pick-up-one-foot-after-another method that had worked on the grass wouldn't work here, so I pushed off across the smooth pavement in a tipsy way. I must have pushed a little too hard, though, because my left leg trailed behind and I almost did a split. And not a very graceful one. The former fourth-grade klutz hadn't disappeared at all. She was just a little bit older.

Oh, why had I let Dad talk me into this today? The sky was too blue and the clouds were too fluffy to expect a quiet park where a person could learn to skate in peace. If I didn't fall down on my own, I definitely would when a biker, runner, or skater whizzed by a little too closely.

"Come on, Pansy!" Andy called back to me. He was miles ahead now.

I rolled to a stop by leaning over and reaching for the ground. This wasn't so difficult since I was barely moving anyway. "Go on ahead!" I yelled to him as I kneeled down on the path. "I'll catch up later!"

Catch up? Ha, ha. Only in my dreams. Soon he'd be back around, catching up with *me* on his second lap.

Which was exactly what happened. I'd fallen twice by then and could already feel a blister popping up on my right ankle.

"Looking good!" Andy said as he clapped me on the shoulder.

Andy's pat was enough to send me to the ground again. That's when I heard the sound of wheels behind me. I stood up bravely, turning to see what was coming.

"Look out!" warned Andy as a skateboarder pulled by three yapping dogs tried to pass me on the left.

I tried to step back out of the way. Instead of rolling backward, I rolled forward. Right into three outstretched leashes. My arms waved around in the air, and I could feel I was losing my balance, so I reached out for the leashes to keep from falling.

The skateboarder jumped off his board. "Whoaa!" he commanded his dogs, which might have meant "stop" in some languages but not in a language the dogs understood.

"Hey, wait, come back here!" the skateboarder yelled when he realized his dogs were no longer pulling him.

They were pulling *me*!

"AAAAHHH!!!" Screams echoed in my ear, and it took a second to realize they were coming from my mouth. The other people on the path turned into a colorful blur as I flew past, clutching the leashes. My heart dropped to my toenails, and I finally got what people meant when they said, "My life flashed before my eyes."

And then the craziest thing happened: the three dogs must have sent ESP messages to each other because together they turned, heading down the hill toward the lake.

"HELPPPP!!!!" I screamed. My Rollerblades hit the uneven ground, and my legs shook as I rolled over rocks and bumps.

"Tiko! Bansai! Moochers!" yelled the skateboarder.

I heard Andy calling my name, but I couldn't answer him. I was being hurled toward my death. I was about to sink into the mucky lake, my Rollerblades sticking out of the water to show where I'd gone. There'd be no Good Citizens party for me because *I'd be dead*. Which, of course, would disappoint Anna once she got better.

I wouldn't be too happy about it, either.

*Get hold of yourself, Pansy!* My logical voice kicked in. I could avoid death and humiliation if I stopped myself before landing in the lake. But how? There was only one thing I could do. And luckily, it was something I was exceptional at. I had to drop the leashes and fall.

So I did.

Everything happened so fast. The earth rushed up to meet me, and I landed face forward with a thump. My hands stung as I sat up and spit out a clump of grass. The dogs turned and circled the lake. The skateboarder didn't stop to ask how I was. He got back on his skateboard and took off after his dogs. "Tiko! Bansai! Moochers!" his voice bellowed into the distance.

*Whoosh!* My breath came out fast, the way air escapes from a bike tire when you hit a nail. My right palm was bleeding, but my kneepads had stayed in place. I wrapped my arms around my knees and rocked back and forth, staring out at the sun reflecting off the lake.

"Wow, you were something!" Andy sounded excited as he dropped down next to me. "You were going really fast!"

I threw my arms around Andy, knocking him to the ground. "I made it!" I yelled. "I faced death, and I survived!"

Andy sat up and laughed. "The lake's only about four feet deep, you know."

"Really?" I brushed hair out of my eyes. "But still. The dogs could have flung me into the lake, and I could have hit my head on a rock. *CRRRACK.* That would have been the end of Pansy Smith."

Andy laughed again. "The end of your Rollerblades, maybe."

I looked down at my skates. Maybe that wouldn't have been such a bad thing.

"Anyway, you did great. You stayed up for a long time."

"Really?"

Andy nodded. "I would have let go a lot quicker than you did. You looked like a pro."

"A pro? Yeah, right," I said with a grin. "Hey, do me a favor."

"What?"

"Promise you'll never tell anyone I got pulled by dogs across Gateway Park and almost ended up in the lake."

Andy laughed.

"I mean it," I said. "Promise?"

Andy shrugged. "Okay. I promise. Though I'd be proud of it if I were you."

We sat on the grass, staring at the water for a few minutes while I caught my breath. Andy got to his feet first. "Come on, let's go around again."

*Again? Wasn't I daring enough for one day?* But I reached for his hand even though I was feeling pretty sore and a bit shaky. This time I made it all the way around with only two falls. It was an improvement, but I'd had enough. I limped over to the nearest bench and pulled off my skates.

Andy sat down next to me. "Are you okay?"

"Sure." I wiggled my toes. Even though I was starting to feel like one big bruise, I decided not to say anything. "We'd better get back to Anna and your mom, though."

We walked slowly back to the playground. "Mom, you should have seen what happened to Pansy!" Andy said when we spotted her on the bench by the swings. "She was sensational! You wouldn't believe it!"

"I wasn't sensational," I said, taking off my helmet.

"It's not every day that someone gets pulled by dogs across Gateway Park," Andy said. "I didn't even know Pansy could skate."

"I can't," I protested.

Mrs. Liddell gave me a quick smile, but I knew she wasn't listening. I watched her brush the hair away from Anna's face. "Anna had a bad seizure just now," she said quietly.

My heart thumped harder than when the dogs were pulling me.

"Another one?" Andy asked. "I thought she had a bad one last night."

"She did. I was hoping she wouldn't have any today."

I kneeled down next to the wheelchair and reached for Anna's hand. Anna must have been asleep because she didn't squeeze back. "Is she all right?"

"She's fine," Mrs. Liddell said. "The seizures just wear her out."

I only nodded, because I didn't know what to say to Mrs. Liddell. Even though it was a warm day, goose bumps popped up on my arms. Mom had explained to me that Anna was having seizures because of the brain damage. She had to wear a special helmet when she walked because if she had a seizure, she'd fall to the ground and pass out—and she could get really hurt.

"I hope you feel better," I whispered to her even though she was sleeping.

"I hate to cut the afternoon short," Andy's mother said. "I was hoping to have a picnic lunch. I packed sandwiches and chips . . ."

"That's okay," I said. "Anna needs to go home." I glanced over at Andy. He shoved his hands in his pockets and kicked a pebble across the pavement.

On the way home, I wanted to say something to make him feel better about Anna's seizures the way he'd made me feel better about my roller-blading. I wanted to tell Andy that the seizures would be all gone once the doctors operated on her brain. But for some reason, I still hadn't told him I'd overheard Mom's phone conversation. As much as I wanted to talk about it, I kept waiting for Andy to bring it up first.

We walked beside each other, taking turns kicking the pebble down the sidewalk. Neither of us said a word all the way home.

## CHAPTER FIVE

# Thirteen Weeks, Six Days

I pushed open the front door and dropped my Roller-blades on the floor with a loud clunk.

"Pansy?" Mom looked up from where she sat eating lunch at the kitchen table. "You're home early. How'd it go?"

"Okay," I said, deciding not to tell her about my adventure with the dogs. "But we had to skip the picnic. Anna had another bad seizure, and they had to go home."

"Is Anna all right?"

"I guess." I sat down next to Mom. "Mrs. Liddell said she gets super tired from the seizures."

"I know. It can take a lot out of a person, going through that all the time." Mom put down her coffee cup and stared straight at me. "There's something I've been meaning to tell you."

"About Anna?" I asked.

Mom nodded. "The Liddells think they know a way to stop the seizures. Or most of them anyway."

A grin stretched across my face. "Do you mean surgery? I already know all about it. Anna's going to have an operation on her brain!"

"How did you find out?"

"I overheard you talking on the phone to Mrs. Liddell last week."

"Honey," Mom said, reaching for my hand. "Look at me."

I did. Mom's mouth was a straight line, and her eyes didn't sparkle with the excitement I felt. When she spoke, her voice was firm and serious. "I need you to listen. The Liddells are considering surgery to help with the seizures. But they can't bring the old Anna back. Do you understand?"

I blinked a few times. Mom squeezed my hand. "I wish I could tell you something different, but there is no cure for brain damage."

*No cure.* The words echoed in my head. I pulled my hand away from Mom's and walked over to the counter. Then I got out the bread and peanut butter and began to make my lunch.

Mom didn't know what she was talking about. Doctors couldn't predict the future. There were new cures for diseases all the time! Scientists had figured out how to make blind and deaf people see and hear, and I'd even read an article in *Scholastic News* about a paralyzed girl who learned to walk again.

Just because Mom said there wasn't a cure didn't mean the surgery wouldn't work for Anna.

"Without seizures, Anna will be much more comfortable," Mom continued. "And she'll be a lot more alert and energetic. Surgery's risky, but it will be a good thing for her."

"I know," I said.

Mom got up and poured a glass of milk for me. "Pansy?"

I sat down at the table with my peanut butter sandwich. "Yeah?"

"If you ever need to talk, you know I'm here for you, right?"

"Yeah." I took a bite of the sandwich. "Can we talk about something else now?"

Mom studied me for a minute, then smiled. "Of course we can. So, tell me all about your morning at the park. Was it a good day for skating?"

***

"Independent Reader starts tomorrow," Miss Quetzel announced on Monday morning. "As part of your reading grade, you'll be required to read one Independent Reader book at your level each month and take a comprehension test on the computer." Miss Quetzel held up a library book and showed us the label on the spine. "For those of you who are new to this program, each book will be marked with a blue label that has the reading level and the amount of points you can earn. You and your parents can look on the school website for a list of all the books that have Independent Reader tests. Now, here's the good news." Miss Quetzel smiled at us. "For every point you earn, you'll have the chance to spend Reading Bucks on some awesome rewards!"

An excited hum filled the room as Miss Quetzel passed around a handout. "Your parents will need to sign this paper, which explains the program and the rewards in detail." I scanned the paper. Bookmarks. Candy. Homework passes. Even better: popsicles in the room at lunch with Miss Quetzel!

"We get to eat in the room?" someone else called out.

"It's up to you if you want to save up your Bucks for popsicles in the room. Some of the other prizes won't cost as much," Miss Quetzel said. "But all of it depends on how much reading you do. There's also the school trophy for the student in each grade who earns the most points. But remember, class, this is not a contest to see who is the smartest. The student who wins the contest is the one who puts the most time and effort into reading. And my goal as a teacher is to encourage *all of you* to become lifelong readers."

While Miss Quetzel explained more about the comprehension tests and the goal of the program, my mind raced. Last year, Anna had tried to earn the most points so she could win a trophy at the awards ceremony at the end of the year. But by January, it was clear she wasn't going to make it. Daniel Walker, a quiet boy who always walked around with his nose in a book, had taken over the first-place spot.

By February, he was so far ahead that Anna stopped racing through books. Now, it was up to me to win this year's trophy. And this was something I could do. I was really good at reading, and I could read pretty fast.

I would win. For both of us.

## CHAPTER SIX

# Twelve Weeks, Two Days

The next day in the school library, I checked out two thick books. But when I got home and started reading, I discovered a new problem. How could I find time to roller-blade every day and also read enough to earn more points than Daniel in the contest? Roller-blade while reading a book at the same time?

I didn't skate all week and finished the first book over the weekend. A few days later, the solution to my skating/ reading problem came to me like a postcard in the mailbox. I'd roller-blade to school instead of waiting for the afternoon! That would give me more time to earn Independent Reader points after school and on the weekend.

"Are you sure about this?" Mom asked me as I sat on the bottom porch step, lacing up my skates. "I don't want you to be late."

"Rollerblades are faster than walking." I stood up. "I'll get there in no time."

"Don't forget your backpack." Mom strapped it over my shoulders. I leaned forward and touched the ground with one hand.

Mom shook her head. "Really, Pansy, there's plenty of time for skating after school. How are you going to make it with that heavy backpack?"

"No problem," I said, standing up tall. "The backpack is great for balance. See you later!" With that, I pushed off with a less than graceful stroke—but I was up on my wheels. And moving a whole lot faster than if I had walked.

"Pansy!" Mom called out. "What about your shoes?"

"I've got them!" I yelled back as I pushed with the other foot.

*Push and swing your arms. Glide. Now the other side. Push and swing your arms. Glide.* Halfway down the block, I was starting to get the hang of it. I had figured out that if you swing the opposite arm back when you push off with your foot, you can really pick up speed . . . which was actually a little fun.

Until I got to the top of the street and turned the corner. My backpack swung to one side, and my feet slipped right out from under me. *Klunk* went my backpack as it hit the ground. *Thwack* went my knee as it struck the concrete.

*Yowwch.* I didn't have to look at my knees and hands to know that they were bleeding. I sat up slowly, brushing the pebbles from my palms. My jeans were torn, and blood was beginning to gush from my wounds.

Well, maybe not gush exactly. But it was definitely a trickle. I hadn't scratched myself up this badly since I was seven, when I played Follow the Leader with Anna and fell off a brick wall.

Of course back then, I cried. Anna made me sit and wait while she ran back to her house to get first aid supplies. Then she cleaned off my knees and stuck the Band-Aids on, just like a real nurse.

I dabbed at my knees and hands with a loose piece of denim, gritting my teeth. Well, there was no one who would magically appear to doctor me up this time. That left me with two choices: roller-blade to Andy's and switch to shoes there, or switch to shoes now. I really wanted a third choice—to sit in this spot the rest of the day. But extraordinary people don't give up.

Extraordinary people are not stupid, either. I took off my skates and switched to my shoes. As I limped down the street to Andy's, I realized I'd forgotten something important when I took off on blades that morning.

Rollerblades are heavy. And they're really heavy in a backpack along with your math book, especially if you've fallen and skinned your knee like you used to do when you were a little kid. Which, by the way, hurt just as badly, but what stinks about being ten-and-a-half is you have to be brave.

"Pansy!" Andy hopped off his porch when he saw me coming and ran over to meet me. "What happened?"

I shrugged. "No big deal." I pulled the backpack off my aching shoulders and handed it to him.

Andy reached for it, then dropped it to the ground. "What's in your backpack? A hundred pounds of rocks?"

"Rollerblades." I hobbled along beside him. "Do you have any Band-Aids?"

"Why are there Rollerblades in your backpack? Why are you limping? How come you need a Band-Aid?"

I let out a long sigh. For a smart kid, Andy sure couldn't add up the clues. I pulled myself up onto his porch and collapsed on the first step. "I started out on Rollerblades. Then I fell." I held up my scratched-up palms and pointed to my torn jeans.

"Okay. Be right back." Andy ran in the house. He came back out with a super-sized Band-Aid for my knee, two smaller ones for my hand, and a bottle of antiseptic. After I cleaned myself up and stuck on the bandages, I pulled out my skates and dropped them on the porch. "I'll just pick them up after school," I told him as we headed down the driveway.

"Whatever you say."

"Makes sense, doesn't it?" I told him. "Why would I want to carry them all the way to school?"

"Beats me," said Andy. "I don't get why you were skating to school anyway."

"For practice. Didn't I tell you Mom said she'll sign me up for ice-skating lessons if I show her I'm serious about it?"

Andy grinned. "You think she'll still sign you up for ice-skating lessons after you come home with torn jeans from roller-blading?"

"She said I have to show I'm motivated. I think I just proved that, don't you?"

"Never knew you wanted to be a champion figure skater."

I smoothed the Band-Aids on my hands. I wanted to tell him the real reason I was killing myself on Roller-blades. But it was hard to explain. "I never said anything about being a champion. I just want to learn to skate, that's all."

"You can't wait until after school?"

I shook my head. "No time for that. I've got a lot of reading to do. Hey, I'll tell you a secret if you promise not to tell."

"Who am I going to tell?"

I leaned over and whispered, "I'm going to be first place in the reading contest."

"What?"

"You heard me. First place. I'm really good at reading, you know."

"Well, yeah, sure. But first place?"

"Why not?"

"Because Daniel Walker's in our class, that's why," Andy said as we approached the entrance of the school.

"So what?"

"Daniel Walker's won the contest for the last two years, that's what."

I stopped and turned to face Andy. "You don't think I can do it?"

"I'm not saying you can't do it. But it won't be easy." He shrugged and walked toward the entrance. "What's the big deal anyway? It's just a dumb contest."

"Maybe to you. But not to me," I said. *Or Anna.* "Besides," I added, "it's not like Daniel's a genius or anything."

"He's not a genius," Andy said. "But the only thing he really does is read."

Andy had a point. Daniel didn't seem to care about friends, he wasn't good at sports, and he didn't appear to have any hobbies. He took a book with him to lunch and to recess. Was I going to have to do the same if I wanted to beat him in the contest?

I was hanging up my backpack, still thinking about the reading contest, when someone rammed me from the side. Like a big solid truck. I turned to find Zach Turansky beside me. He narrowed his eyes and pushed me out of the way with his broad shoulders.

I would have pushed back, except the truth is, I was aching all over. My shoulders. My knees. My ankles. My arms and legs. Even my chin hurt, even though I couldn't remember hitting it.

I leaned down to adjust the Band-Aid on my knee, forgetting all about Zach.

"Hey, Klutz," he bent over, his stinky breath washing over my face. "What'd you do, trip over your own feet on the way to school?"

I straightened up, squared my shoulders, and gave him my best glare. That was it. On this particular day, that was the bravest I could be.

Zach sneered. Then he said with a rough laugh, "Maybe you should get a wheelchair like your retard friend Anna. Might keep you from tearing up your jeans."

My eyes misted over, and I balled up my fists, even though my palms stung. I wanted to yell, "Anna isn't retarded! She is waaay smarter than you could ever dream to be!"

But I couldn't get a word out. I spun away from him and limped off to my seat, thinking about what happened after Anna went into the hospital last spring. When we returned after break, the school counselor, Mrs. Levin, spoke to the whole class while Andy was out of the room. She explained all about how Anna had caught meningitis and how her brain didn't send the right messages anymore.

"It's one of those rare cases where a perfectly healthy person becomes infected, and it leads to a severe brain injury," Mrs. Levin had told the class. "Andy and his family need our thoughts and prayers right now. Anna has survived a very serious illness, but there are a lot of challenges ahead."

I had sat at my desk, my hands clasped tightly in my lap while the counselor spoke. My throat had felt tight and dry as Mrs. Levin called on people and tried to answer their questions.

Later that day, I had noticed that kids were staring at me and whispering to each other. But no one asked me how it felt to have your best friend become brain damaged. And no one asked Andy how it felt to have a twin sister who'd turned into someone else.

I think people were scared to say anything to me or Andy right after it happened. But a few weeks later, Andy turned Zach's name in to the teacher when he was the room monitor. Zach had been throwing paper airplanes around the room and making everyone laugh, and Zach had to miss recess that afternoon.

The first time Zach called Andy "twin retard" was soon after that. But he always made his comments about Anna in a very quiet voice, like he was afraid to get caught. I never hated anyone before. But I hated Zach Turansky with all my heart.

The bell rang and brought me back from my daydream. Miss Quetzel said, "Let's start with our speed drills this morning to get them out of the way. Those of you who've finished through the twelves, please take out a book and read silently."

Twelves? People had already made it all the way to twelve? I was still on three. Three!

I heard Madison take her book out of her desk, but I stopped thinking about everything except the quiz. I stared down at my torn jeans as I waited for Miss Quetzel to tell us to begin. I raced through my three times tables, finishing before Miss Quetzel called, "Time."

I put down my pencil and smiled. My hands didn't even sting anymore. Tomorrow morning, I'd skate to Andy's house again. And this time, I'd bring my own Band-Aids.

## CHAPTER SEVEN

# Twelve Weeks, One Day

"Want to come over this afternoon?" Andy asked me at recess on Thursday.

I climbed to the top of the monkey bars and sat down next to him in our usual recess spot, my knees still stiff from the crash the day before. But I'd found a solution. Knee pads! Yesterday I found an old pair in the basement, and this morning they worked like a charm. I turned to Andy. "Sorry," I told him. "I have Girl Scouts this afternoon."

Andy's mouth dropped open. "Girl Scouts?" he managed to say, as if I'd just announced I was taking off on a spaceship to another galaxy.

I tucked my hair behind my ear. "We're meeting in the media center after school."

"Since when did you become interested in Girl Scouts?"

"Since now. The flier came home yesterday, and I told my parents I wanted to join."

Andy snorted.

"What's wrong with Girl Scouts? You're in Boy Scouts, aren't you?"

Andy shrugged. "Well, sure. I've been in Boy Scouts since first grade. But I like camping. You're the one who freaks out about bugs."

"So maybe I've changed."

"You?" Andy let out a laugh, but it wasn't a real one.

I crossed my arms in front of my chest. "I can join Girl Scouts if I want to."

Andy looked off into the distance. I turned away from him, too, staring out at the rest of the playground. An autumn breeze blew orange and golden leaves from the trees. You could see just about everything going on from our spot on top of the jungle gym. There was the regular group of boys playing basketball on the court, kids playing kickball on the field, some playing tag, others on the swings and climbing equipment. I spotted Madison and a group of girls walking around the outside of the play area, talking.

Up until last December, Andy used to hang out with his best friend, James Olivio, at recess. They didn't usually join the games, but they'd sit on the monkey bars or under a tree with their notebooks, sharing comic strips they'd drawn. Like Andy, James was into art and building stuff, and sometimes we'd all play in the Liddell tree house after school, creating imaginary worlds.

But James moved to Florida after winter break, and that's when Andy starting hanging out with me and Anna more. He wasn't interested in running around at recess with the other boys, and I sure was glad to have Andy after Anna got sick, or I would have been completely alone. But sometimes I wondered if Andy wished he had another boy to hang out with instead of just me.

"You never joined Girl Scouts when Anna asked you to," Andy said quietly.

*That's why I'm doing it now*, I thought. But I didn't say it aloud. I turned to face him. "That was last year. I'm different now. People can change, you know."

"I bet Madison Poplin is in Girl Scouts," Andy said.

"She is, but—"

"I knew it." Andy jumped down from the bars.

"What's that supposed to mean?" I asked, climbing down after him.

Andy didn't answer me. "I think I'll go check out the kickball game," he said, even though I knew it wasn't one of his favorite things to do.

I watched as he wandered off toward the field, leaving me on the playground all by myself. Madison waved as she walked past, but she didn't ask if I'd join them. So I sat down on an empty swing and pumped back and forth, thinking about why I simply had to join Girl Scouts. And it had nothing to do with Madison Poplin.

Last year, I'd promised Anna I'd go to Girl Scout sleep-away camp with her in the mountains for a whole week during spring break, even though neither of us had ever been to sleep-away camp before.

I could hear Mrs. Liddell's voice inside my head: "You'll have such great time! You'll go kayaking, rappelling, hiking, camping under the stars . . ."

Here's the truth: it never sounded like such a great time to me. Because all I could think about was getting up in the middle of the night and walking to the bathroom in the pitch dark. A bathroom that would be full of all kinds of creepy bugs I did not want to meet.

Mom jumped on board right away, saying what a terrific adventure it would be for the two of us. You'd think she would have warned me to think about it carefully before making any promises. She certainly knew how I felt about bugs and being alone in the dark. But then Anna started talking about how much fun we'd have together, roasting marshmallows and catching snails in the creek and giggling all night in our sleeping bags. For a whole month, I went right along with her, making lists of what we'd bring and planning all the exciting things we'd do.

Three days before the trip, I quit faking it. I told my parents there was no way I was going. They tried to get me to change my mind, but for hours and hours, I begged and pleaded with them not to send me to that horrible place. Boy, were they disappointed in me.

"Pansy," my dad said, "you can't let your fears overtake your life."

"Not to mention the fact that you're letting down a friend," Mom added. "How are you going to explain this to Anna?"

It wasn't easy, that's for sure.

"I can't believe it!" Anna said when I broke the news. Her cheeks turned bright red. "How could you do this to me?"

I tried to tell her that I was having nightmares about going. That I was scared to death of sleeping in a tent in the dark with wild animals all around. And most of all that I didn't want to go to the bathroom in a place with fuzzy spiders on the walls. (I'd been to one of those bath houses when we took a day trip to the mountains, and I can tell you there are fuzzy spiders in all the corners. And I had to hold it until we found a fast-food restaurant on the way home.)

Anna usually understood if I backed out of something because I was scared. But this time, she wasn't listening to any of it. She squinched her eyes up and glared at me in a not very friendly way. "But you *promised*. Best friends shouldn't break their promises."

My eyes filled with tears. "I'm sorry, I really am. I can't help it!"

"You *can* help it, Pansy. And it's not the first time you've gone back on your promise either."

I shook my head. "That's not true! I always keep my promises."

"Really? You're always saying you'll do things, and then you change your mind."

"Like what?"

"Like when we signed up for ice-skating lessons and you quit after *one* lesson."

I shrugged. "Well, yeah. That's because I stink at it."

"You only tried one time! And how about when you said you'd ride The Twister with me at Six Flags, and we stood in line forever, and when it was our turn, I had to ride it by myself?"

"I got scared—"

"Okay. I've got an even worse one. What about last month when you promised to get your hair cut for Locks of Love?" Anna ran her hand across her short bob.

"Oh, yeah." I twisted a long strand of hair around my finger and looked down at my feet. "I really wanted to. I just . . . chickened out."

"I'm tired of you chickening out." Anna crossed her arms in front of her chest. "It's not a good excuse. Especially not this time, when I'm stuck going to camp all by myself. We were supposed to have all kinds of fun together. And now it won't be any fun at all."

"I'm sorry!" I said again, and this time the tears spilled from under my lashes and slipped down my cheeks. "I really wanted to go with you, but I—just—can't!"

Anna rolled her eyes. "Tell it to someone else," she said, waving me away. "Maybe you better tell it to your new best friend, because I'm sick of it." And then Anna stood up, walked me to the door, and did something she'd never done before. She told me to leave.

The worst part about it is that I did. I didn't know what else to do. I walked right out without another glance at her, and she slammed the door behind me.

The next time I saw her was in the hospital. And that's why I headed to the media center for the Girl Scout meeting after school. To prove to Anna that I could face things I was scared of, and when she got better, I'd make it up to her by going with her to sleep-away camp.

As I walked down the hall after school, I realized Madison and Emma were right in front of me. Unfortunately, Hannah must have decided that Girl Scouts sounded like a terrific idea, too, because there she was, sticking to Madison like Silly Putty on a hot car seat.

Madison stopped and turned around to face me. "Are you going to the meeting?"

I nodded. "Have you been in Girl Scouts a long time?"

"We've been together since Daisies," Madison said, pointing to Emma and Hannah.

"Last year, I sold the most cookies in the whole troop," Hannah said.

"Well, I love to *eat* Girl Scout cookies," I said. "So I thought I should join this year."

No one laughed at my joke, but Madison smiled. "Eating cookies is my favorite thing, too. Even though I don't really have time for all the selling."

"Me neither." I stopped in the middle of the hall. I hadn't even thought about selling cookies. How was I going to fit in cookie booths along with skating practice, reading, and trying to earn an A-honor-roll ribbon for the first time?

"Come on," Madison said, hooking her arm with mine. "Girl Scouts is not just about cookies."

Hannah turned her nose up in the air and walked ahead of us. I fell in step beside Madison as we walked toward the media center.

"It's wonderful to see a room full of such lovely girls," a tall blonde-haired woman said a few minutes later. "My name is Mrs. Kendricks, and I'll be one of the troop leaders this year."

"She's Melanie Kendricks's mom," Madison whispered to me. "She was our leader last year, too."

Mrs. Kendricks seemed to have all the right qualifications for a Girl Scout troop leader: a big smile, hair that bobbed back and forth while she talked, and enthusiasm! enthusiasm! enthusiasm! At one point during her speech, I thought she might jump up on a chair and do a split jump in the air while shouting, "Hooray for Girl Scouts!"

By the time she was done talking, Mrs. Kendricks had erased the doubts from my head. Well, most of them, anyway. There were still a few left, like the smudge of a dry erase marker you can still see on the board after you've erased the words. There was that tiny voice inside that kept saying, "Come on, Pansy! You know you'd hate sitting at a table in front of the grocery store selling cookies. And no matter how fantastic Mrs. Kendricks makes it sound to spend the night outside under the stars singing campfire songs, there are still those creepy bugs . . . and walking to the bath house by yourself in the middle of the night."

I shut out the voice, thinking about Anna sitting next to me instead. She'd have a big grin on her face. "I'm so glad you're joining, too!" she'd say to me. "We're going to have so much fun together. I can't wait for the camping trip. It's going to be awesome!"

"Are you going to join?" Madison asked an hour later as we sat on a bench, waiting for our rides. Hannah and Emma had already been picked up, so it was just the two of us.

"Yeah," I said. "It sounds like fun."

Madison smiled. "Great! What Try-It badge do you want to work on?"

"Mom usually doesn't let me near the kitchen, so maybe cooking. Or crafts. Like jewelry making?"

"Ooh, I love making jewelry. Have you ever been to Beadopoly?"

I shook my head. Mom said the prices at Beadopoly were like highway robbery, so she never let me go there.

"We go to Beadopoly all the time," Madison said. "Mom always makes something for herself. I made this one last weekend." She showed me her bracelet with blue and pink glittery beads.

"It's pretty," I said. "Mom won't let me earn a jewelry badge if I have to go to a place like Beadopoly, though."

Madison laughed. "Girl Scouts won't let you earn a badge that way. They're all about doing it yourself. Like making your own beads out of clay and painting them. Or making bracelets from shells you find on the beach."

"I'm pretty good at that," I told her.

"Me too," Madison said. "I love making crafts. Hey, maybe we should work on our badges together! You can come to my house to do the baking, and we can go to your house and work on the jewelry."

I hesitated. Madison Poplin was asking me if I wanted to come over and work on badges with *her*? Anna would be back in a few months, so making a new friend wasn't really part of my plan.

"What do you think, Pansy?" she asked again.

Madison had been in Girl Scouts for a couple years and certainly knew her way around earning badges. I was new to all of it and besides, Anna wouldn't mind.

"Okay," I finally said as Mom's Honda pulled up in front of the school. "Sure."

"Great," Madison said with a grin. "See you tomorrow!"

I waved at her as I climbed in the car. With Madison helping me, I could do this. And maybe, just maybe, it wouldn't be so hard after all.

## CHAPTER EIGHT

# Eleven Weeks, Two Days

Something amazing happened over the next week as I skated to Andy's every morning wearing my knee pads. At first I thought it was luck that kept me from wiping out like I had that first day. But then it began to feel like something else. Could it be . . . was I actually *learning to roller-blade?* There wasn't much to it, after all. Push and glide, push and glide . . .

My feet and legs began to feel steadier, and even when I fell, I went down easily instead of crashing to the ground.

And then one morning, about a week after I'd started skating to school, I made it all the way to Andy's *without a single fall!*

"Woohoo!" I pumped my arms and cheered as I clambered up Andy's porch.

"What are you so excited about?" he asked me.

"You are now looking at Rollerblader Extraordinaire," I told him with a grin.

Andy laughed. "How'd you win that title?"

"Stayed up on my wheels the whole way here," I said as I pulled off my skates. "I figure I'm onto something. Who knows what I'll conquer next?"

Andy shook his head. "You never know."

It turns out he was right. When we entered the classroom, Miss Quetzel had posted the first round of Independent Reader scores on the wall.

"Wow, you're in third place!" Andy said.

I blinked a few times and traced my finger carefully from my name to the points, just to be sure. Yup, there it was on the computer print-out after two weeks of reading: PANSY SMITH: 10 POINTS, RANK: 3. Daniel was at the top of the list, of course. But he was only ahead by *four points*.

"Great job!" Madison said, putting her hand on my shoulder. "You earned almost as many points as Daniel Walker!"

"How'd you do it?" Hannah asked. "Your mother must let you stay up late reading."

"Not really." I glanced at the list for Hannah's ranking: 15. "I'm a fast reader, though."

Hannah muttered something under her breath.

I stared at the print-out. *I can do this. Give me a few more weeks, and I'll have more points than Daniel, more than anyone in the fifth grade.*

"I know how Pansy got those points." Zach's voice broke through my thoughts. "I bet she didn't read any of those books. She watched the movies instead!"

I spun around to face him. "That's not true! I read every page of each of those books. If you think you can watch movies to earn points, then why do you only have . . ." I scanned the list quickly. "One point?"

That brought some giggles. Zach was at the bottom of the list!

"You got a problem with it?" He pushed some of the other kids aside so he was standing right next to me. Then he squinted his beady eyes at me, like a hawk waiting to pounce on his prey. "You got something to say, then you better spit it out."

I swallowed hard. "No, I—I—"

The crowd surrounding the Independent Reader list grew quiet.

"Yeah, I knew it." Zach threw back his shoulders. A mean grin stretched across his face. "You're a fake. Everyone will find out soon enough." He turned and strutted to his seat before I could get another word out.

My cheeks blazed, and I stared down at my mismatched shoes.

Andy nudged me. "Don't worry about it," he whispered. "No one listens to anything Turansky says."

I shrugged and trudged slowly to my seat. The truth was that Andy was wrong. *Everyone* listened to Zach Turansky, and no one ever argued with him.

I read all those books and didn't watch a single movie. But I had read one of them the month before school started. Miss Quetzel had said they needed to be books we read this school year, not in the past. It had only been a few weeks before school started . . . but did I really deserve all those points?

As I started on my morning work, all I could hear was Zach's voice in my head: *Pansy Smith is a big fake.*

A few minutes later, we took our speed drills. I'd passed threes and fours, which was something like a miracle. This was my first day on fives, and I should have sped through it. Fives are the easiest of all. I finished the drill before Miss Quetzel called time, but I'd made two mistakes.

The rest of the morning wasn't any better. I got caught on the wrong page during a social studies lesson and answered the wrong problem while we were checking our math homework. The second time Miss Quetzel caught me not paying attention, she paused and stared at me like she'd just sucked on a lemon. I held my breath a minute, afraid she'd take away from the Good Citizens point chart. But she just shook her head as a warning and moved on.

Extraordinary people didn't get lemon faces from their teachers. They didn't make stupid mistakes on the five times tables, the easiest quiz of all. They didn't cheat, either. And they would never let a stupid person like Zach get under their skin.

*** 

"You know what, Pansy?" Madison said at lunch. "I think if you really try, you can earn more points than Daniel Walker."

"If I keep reading and Daniel keeps reading, then we'll stay exactly the same," I said.

"Daniel probably isn't thinking about the contest, though. He's just reading like he usually does. It'll be like a surprise attack. You speed up, he stays at the same speed . . ." Madison snapped her fingers. "And all of a sudden you're in the lead. Daniel wouldn't even see it coming."

"Hmmm." I thought about that for a minute. "You really think I can take the lead?"

"I'm sure of it," Madison said with a grin.

"I doubt it," Hannah said. "Daniel's the best reader in the school."

I glanced over at Andy. He was busy spooning ravioli out of his thermos, like he didn't even hear the conversation.

"Pansy can do it," Madison said, and this time I grinned back at her.

By the time I got home from school, I'd forgotten all about Zach. Maybe Madison was right. I'd have to work extra hard, and it would take some luck, but it wouldn't be impossible.

"Mom!" I yelled as I burst in the door. "Guess what! I'm in third place in Independent Reader, and I'm only four points from the top of the list!"

"That's wonderful!" Mom said as she put a bowl of Chex Mix and a glass of milk on the table.

I dropped my backpack with my heavy skates and the mismatched shoe onto the ground; I always remembered to change back to matching shoes before walking inside the house. "Madison thinks I can make it to first place if I keep trying."

"Madison sounds like a smart girl. You can do whatever you want if you try your best." I scooped a handful of Chex Mix and poured it in my mouth, thinking about what she said.

"How's the skating coming?" Mom asked me. "I just got an email that the next session at the Ice Palace starts in two weeks."

"You won't believe this. Today, I made it to Andy's without falling."

"Terrific! Sounds like you're ready to hit the ice-skating rink."

"Really? You'll sign me up for lessons?"

"Sure," Mom said. "I told you if you practiced on Rollerblades, we'd enroll you in lessons. I can sign you up online tonight, if you want."

"Awesome!" I leaped out of my seat and threw my arms around her neck. Everything was working out after all. I was third place in the reading contest, I learned to roller-blade without falling, and Mom was signing me up for ice-skating lessons.

So far, I was following through on all my promises. Anna was going to be amazed at me when she got better.

## CHAPTER NINE

# Ten Weeks, Six Days

I had big plans for the weekend. On Saturday morning, I got up before eight. I'd checked out two books from the school library, each worth three points. My plan was to read one book on Saturday; on Sunday, the other.

I thumbed through the first novel. It had twenty chapters. As I thought about how many chapters I needed to read before breakfast, there was a knock on my door.

Dad poked his head inside. "Glad to see you're up already. Guess where we're going today."

I looked up from my book. "Where?"

"Stone Mountain. The weather's perfect, your mom's making her famous pimento cheese sandwiches . . . What do you say?"

"I can't wait!" I leaped from the bed, and the book landed open-faced on top of my Rollerblades, which were lying on the floor. "Can I invite Andy?"

"Sure. We're leaving around ten."

I forgot all about my weekend reading plan as I called Andy. I was so happy when he said he wanted to come, too. Ever since I'd joined Girl Scouts, Andy and I had gotten along okay. But I'd been so busy reading and skating that we hardly saw each other outside of school.

When I ran back to my room to grab my sweatshirt, I tripped over the book that had fallen on the floor. That reminded me of the goal I'd set for the weekend: read two books, even if it killed me.

I sighed and tucked the book under my arm as I ran out to the car.

"What are you reading?" Andy asked a few minutes later.

"*The Best Day Ever.*" I showed him the cover.

"Is it a mystery?"

I shook my head.

"Fantasy? Sci-fi?"

I shook my head again.

"What's it about then?"

I shrugged. "I'm only on the first page. So far, it's not about much."

"Then why'd you bring it in the car if it's not even good enough to tell me about?"

"It's for Independent Reader," I answered, as though that explained everything. Andy loved to read as much as I did, and usually we liked the same books.

He looked at me as if I'd lost my mind. "You picked it because it's for Independent Reader, even if it stinks?"

"Well, I don't know that for sure yet. It's worth three points, and I need to read two books this weekend if I want to get near first place."

"First place?" Dad piped in from the front seat. "Whatever happened to reading for fun? All I ever hear about lately is points, points, points!"

"Well, I think it's great," Mom said. "If this reading program motivates you to read more, Pansy, then there's nothing wrong with that."

"Yeah," I said, glad to have Mom on my side. "But it's not going to be easy catching up with Daniel."

"Why do you even care?" Andy asked. "You never cared about it before."

*I'm doing it for Anna!* I wanted to shout. But they wouldn't get it at all.

"I can do it," I finally said. "A lot of people might not believe it, but I think I can make it to first place."

"Of course you can do it!" Dad said, and everyone else chimed in. "That's not what anyone was trying to say."

"How's Anna doing?" Mom asked Andy, changing the subject as I started to dig into the book, which wasn't very interesting after all.

I looked over at Andy. He had that uncomfortable look on his face again, the one he always had whenever anyone mentioned Anna. "She's okay."

"Tell your mom I found a high-protein milkshake for that new diet Anna's on," Mom said. "I've tried it, and it's delicious."

"What new diet?" I asked.

"Anna has to eat lots of protein," Andy said. "Like egg whites and cream and liver."

"Liver?" I wrinkled up my nose. "Yuck!"

"It's supposed to help with her seizures," Mom said.

"She has to eat a lot of gross stuff," Andy said.

"Does she like it?" I asked Andy.

He shrugged. "She eats it. It doesn't smell too good, that's for sure."

I nodded. Anna was tougher and way braver than me, even now.

Andy leaned over and whispered to me, "I've been having dreams that Anna is talking to me."

"What does she say?" I whispered back.

"I can't remember exactly. But she did say, 'I'm right here.'"

"Anna's trying to tell you that she knows what's going on!" I said, forgetting to whisper. "That she understands everything!"

Andy nodded again. Then he smiled. I was bursting to ask him about the surgery, since he still hadn't mentioned it. But I needed to wait until we weren't within earshot of my parents.

I snapped my book shut. For the rest of the ride, we played The Alphabet Game, The License Plate Game, and Count the Cows. I won all three, so maybe I was closer to being extraordinary than I thought.

"I brought my notebook," Andy said after we finished the second round of The Alphabet Game. He turned to a page with the words ZERACLOP CITY at the top. My heart raced. The words were written in Anna's handwriting.

"I think we should build it," Andy said. "I've added some new sketches."

I stared down at the first page full of sketches that Anna, Andy, and I had come up with right before The Big Fight. Anna's the one who came up with the name "Zeraclop," but a lot of the detailed ideas were mine. Andy and I had played with LEGO bricks together all summer, building all kinds of things. But this was the first time either of us had mentioned Zeraclop.

Andy flipped to the page with his new sketches and started talking away about his new plans. He was right. We should build it, for Anna. Her eyes would light up when she saw how hard we'd worked.

I got caught up in the plans, and before I knew it, we had arrived at Stone Mountain.

We stopped at the map board to look at our trail choices. The hiking routes ranged from moderate to strenuous.

"So, what do you think?" Dad asked us. "Is anyone up for the Stone Mountain Loop?"

I looked at the red lines on the map and the key: 4.5 miles of hiking described as "more difficult." I looked over at Andy. He grinned just as I did.

"I want to see the waterfalls!" we both said at the same time. The one-mile loop to the lower and middle falls had always been Anna's favorite, too.

"I think the kids have the right idea," Mom agreed. "That will leave time for us to visit the homestead afterward."

"Looks like I've been outvoted," Dad said as we started on the trail.

My feet crunched on dead leaves as we made our way through the woods, crossing a run-down bridge over a small stream.

"Hey, let's play Poohsticks," I said. Andy and I both grabbed sticks and threw them over on one side of the bridge. Then we ran to the other side and watched to see whose stick would come out first. We'd been playing the game together since we first came to Stone Mountain back in preschool. Anna had always picked just the right kind of sticks, the ones that had enough weight to get past the rocks but weren't so heavy that they'd get stuck.

"Hey, look," Andy said as both sticks sailed past us on the sparkling water, side by side. "It's a tie!"

We played a little while longer until Dad told us to move on. After a few more minutes on the wooded path, we came to a clearing. Another path cut through a meadow full of wildflowers, tall grasses, and brightly colored butterflies. We'd picked the perfect day for hiking. The sky was clear and blue, the sun was just the right amount of hot, and a cool breeze blew back my hair and ruffled through my shirt.

"Remember when we came last fall?" I asked Andy. "It was really hot, and by the time we got to the waterfalls, we all wanted to jump in."

"Yeah," Andy said. "It was about 110 degrees, but we thought it would be cooler here—"

"But it wasn't. We were burning up. Your mom brought frozen water bottles so we could stay cool, remember?"

Andy nodded.

"We had a lot of fun," I said, "even though I thought we might get heatstroke." I giggled. When Andy didn't laugh, too, I looked over at him. His jaw was set firmly as though he was concentrating hard on the trail ahead.

I thought about how both of our families had always gone on day trips together, but everything was so different now. You couldn't push a wheelchair on a trail in the mountains.

"It's too bad your parents couldn't have come with us," I said.

Andy shrugged and looked at the ground.

*In the spring they'll come with us,* I wanted to say. *And Anna will win Poohsticks, like always, and she'll be the first one down the steps to the falls.*

But I kept my words inside. Maybe I was afraid to say them out loud, afraid they would just disappear as soon as they were out of my mouth—as if by telling someone else how I felt, I might keep my hopes from coming true.

We continued to walk in silence, deep in our own thoughts. Soon we could hear the waterfalls ahead. Andy's the one who ran past me this time, the first one to the stone steps that took us down to the Lower Falls.

Roped off beside us, rushing water ran over huge rocks. A sign warned us that if anyone crossed over the ropes, it could lead to "imminent death."

A chill ran up and down as I remembered the way Anna used to lean over the ropes more than she should have, laughing about the sign. Her parents always had to tell her to step back, warning her about the danger.

I was always the most careful about keeping my distance.

I followed Andy down the steps with my parents right behind us. The water roared in my ears once we got to the bottom. We stopped, watching the clear water cascade over the rocks, splashing and frothing its way into a deep pool at the bottom.

"Wow. I'd almost forgotten how it takes your breath away." Mom pulled out her camera to snap some pictures.

The rest of us did the same. Then I put my camera down and stood there, almost hypnotized as the water moved with a power of its own, tumbling over the rocks. I didn't want to leave, but when Mom told us it was time for lunch, my stomach started rumbling, and I realized I was starving.

We headed back up the steps and finished the loop, setting up our picnic in a shady spot. As I bit into my pimento cheese sandwich, I heard a rustle in the woods behind me.

I turned to see a deer standing on the other side of the path. "Look! Oh, she's beautiful!"

"There's more of them, right behind her." Andy got up from the picnic table and stepped closer to the path.

I tiptoed next to him. There were four of them now, the ones in the back moving slowly and quietly through the woods. The one in the front—the one I noticed first—stood perfectly still.

I sucked in my breath. The doe was almost magical, like something out of a fantasy book. I wouldn't have been surprised if she sprouted wings and flew up into the sky.

"Wow . . ." The deer stared back at me with big eyes. Eyes that reminded me of Anna's. Somehow, I felt in my heart that Anna knew what was going on, even if no one else could tell, and she knew she was going to get better. It was something you couldn't explain with words—it was something you had to just believe.

I glanced over at Andy, remembering how he'd told me about his dream where Anna had spoken to him.

I knew that Andy believed. And so did I.

The deer moved her head and blinked. Then she turned and, with a few graceful leaps, she was gone.

## CHAPTER TEN

# Ten Weeks, Four Days

I stared at the computer screen at school Monday morning after my score was posted. I couldn't believe it. I blinked and stared again. The number was still there. A 60. I'd almost flunked the test for *The Best Day Ever*!

Maybe it had something to do with the fact that I waited until Sunday to read the book, and it was boring as can be. I daydreamed during the really slow parts, and I stayed up too late trying to finish it.

My feet dragged as I walked to my seat before the bell rang. I glanced over at Daniel, who grinned at me. There's no way he scored anything as low as a 60 on either of his tests. It was time to face facts: it was almost impossible to beat Daniel. If I wanted to take over the lead, I needed a plan.

I thought about it all through morning math class, even while Miss Quetzel handed out our fractions worksheet. The paper looked like it was for second or third graders because of the drawings. At the top was an image of bunnies eating pizza.

But just because the worksheet looked easy didn't mean I knew how to answer any of the questions.

I was staring down at the silly bunnies when it hit me. *Pictures!* I would check out a picture book every day along with a novel. I'd be more careful in choosing good novels, and then I'd find a picture book that I could read in ten minutes. I'd rack up five extra points, maybe more, each week!

Daniel didn't walk around at recess reading books for little kids, so I'd be sure to beat him. For a second I felt a pang of guilt. Was it cheating if I earned more points by reading easy books?

I glanced over in Daniel's direction. He sat hunched over his desk, his dark hair flopping down over his forehead and across his eyes the way it often did. Something about the way he was sitting, his chin resting on his hand as he leaned forward, made me suspicious.

I took a closer look, spotting the open book propped up inside his desk.

Well! If Daniel Walker could rack up points when he was supposed to be learning about fractions, then I could certainly read a few picture books in my spare time without feeling guilty.

Andy kicked me under my desk. I jumped. "What?"

Andy pointed in Miss Quetzel's direction.

"Oh," I mumbled under my breath. Then I sat up tall in my seat and looked straight at Miss Quetzel. "Can you please repeat the question?"

I heard some snorts and snickers behind me. Zach, no doubt, who never knew the answers when he was called on. And maybe Hannah, too, who *thought* she knew all the answers.

"I asked you how many pieces would be left if the bunnies ate one-third of the pizza?"

I hesitated. Since I hadn't been listening to most of the fractions lesson, I didn't have a clue as to the answer. If I gave the wrong answer to such a simple question, I definitely wouldn't be extraordinary at all.

But maybe there was a way out. I studied the picture. Three little ducklings waddled in the background. "Um, none, Miss Quetzel. Because of those ducklings over there. They would wipe out the rest of the pieces."

The class burst into laughter. It wasn't the making-fun-of-you kind, either. Luckily, Miss Quetzel looked like she was trying hard to keep from smiling, too. "I suppose that's possible. Well, all this talk about pizza reminds me it's time for snack. Finish the worksheet for homework tonight," she said over the slamming of books and chatter as everyone prepared for a break. "I expect mathematically correct answers, whether they are logical or not. Does everyone understand? Pansy, that includes you."

I nodded. That joke had just rolled off my tongue. Even if it wasn't the best joke in the world, it had kept everyone from knowing that I wasn't paying attention. I glanced over at Andy. He was staring at me, his eyebrows wrinkled as if he were thinking hard.

"What?" I asked as I shoved my book into my desk and pulled out my snack.

"I was wondering . . . I know ducks eat stale bread if you toss it at them. But they don't really eat pizza, do they?"

"Well, bunnies don't eat pizza, either. Ducks would probably like it more than rabbits would."

Andy shook his head. "It would probably make them sick. You know, like those signs at the park that read, 'Don't feed the ducks.' It gives them upset stomachs. That's why there's duck poop all over the park." He raised one eyebrow at me. "You might have even landed in some of that duck poop when you were skating around the lake."

I rolled my eyes. Andy knew I'd been joking when I answered the math question, that I didn't really think bunnies or ducks would eat pizza. But here he was, trying to let me know he thought I'd said something really stupid. Why couldn't he have just said, "Great joke, Pansy. If it weren't for you, we'd be doing math until lunchtime"?

"I did not land in any duck poop," I said a little louder than I planned.

I heard a giggle behind me.

"Hey," Madison said, tapping me on the shoulder. "Is it true that ducks eat pizza?"

I turned around. "If it has anchovies on it, they'll eat it."

Madison giggled again. Andy scowled. What was with him these days? Well, if he wanted to be grouchy about the whole thing, that was his problem. I turned to Madison and offered her some of my yogurt-covered pretzels.

"Yum," Madison said, reaching for a handful. "How'd you know they're my favorite?"

"They're my favorite, too!" I said, popping some into my mouth. Andy took his snack out of his desk, turning away from both of us as he bit into an apple.

I turned back to Madison, who was telling me about the pet bunny she hoped her parents would buy her for her birthday.

"The kind with the floppy ears?" I asked her.

"They're called lop-ear bunnies," Madison said. "I don't care what color it is, as long as it has long ears. I'm going to train mine to use the litter box, and I'll let her run around my room. She can even sleep in my bed."

"I wish I could have a lop-ear bunny, too," I told her.

## CHAPTER ELEVEN

# Ten Weeks, Two Days

I'm going to Andy's!" I called to Mom as I rushed back out of the house after school with an armful of supplies for Zeraclop City. I was surprised when Andy asked me on the way home if I wanted to come over, especially after the way he'd acted that morning. I figured it was his way of apologizing, so I jumped at the chance to work on Zeraclop City, even though I needed to practice my skating and I had a seven-point book to read.

I ran the whole way to the Liddells', then knocked my special knock on their front door: *KNOCK KNOCK knock tap.*

"Hi, Pansy," Mrs. Liddell greeted me. "We haven't seen you around here in a while."

"I know. I've been busy with school and stuff." I glanced around the living room. "Where's Anna?"

"She's resting," Mrs. Liddell said. "She has a bronchial infection, so it's probably best if you don't visit right now."

"Oh, I'm not worried about germs," I said, heading down the hall. Mom always told me I had the immune system of an Olympic athlete, which meant I didn't get sick very often.

But Mrs. Liddell followed and caught my arm as I was about to enter Anna's room. "We're trying not to expose *her* to any extra germs," she said. "The doctor wants her to build up her strength over the next few months."

I paused and turned to face her. "Because of the surgery?"

Mrs. Liddell nodded. "Your mom told you it's for the seizures?"

I avoided her eyes. "Um, yeah. She said it would help."

"Well, the doctors are certainly hopeful."

I liked the word *hopeful*, but I didn't tell Mrs. Liddell that. Instead I peeked inside Anna's room. She was lying in bed, her eyes half-closed. Her thick copper hair fanned out over a white pillow. A Disney movie was playing on the television, but she wasn't watching it.

"Hi, Anna," I called to her softly.

When Anna didn't move, I figured she was asleep. I closed my eyes, picturing her old white canopy bed in my mind. It had the most beautiful lavender curtains that would open and close. Whenever I spent the night at Anna's, we'd wait until everyone had gone to bed, and then we'd sneak Oreos from the kitchen, race back to her room, and jump on the bed, exploding into giggles as we closed the curtains around us.

I opened my eyes and stared at Anna where she lay quietly on her bed. After Anna had the stroke, her parents got rid of the canopy bed. They had to buy a bed like the kind in hospitals that you can move up and down easily. It looked cold. Hard. The kind of bed that says sickness all over it.

Anna turned her head in my direction and opened her eyes all the way.

"I'm sorry you're not feeling well," I told her from the doorway. "Your mom wants me to stay out here, so I don't give you any more germs."

Anna stared at me with unblinking eyes. She didn't smile, but I could tell she was listening.

"Come on, Pansy," Andy said as he ran up behind me. "Did you bring any shoeboxes?"

"On the table," I told him. I wanted to stay and talk to Anna. So far I hadn't told her about my goals—I'd been so busy I'd barely seen her since school started.

"Are you coming, or what?" Andy said again, so I waved to Anna and followed Andy down the hall.

"I've got an awesome idea," he said. "We'll cover the shoeboxes with construction paper. Those will be the government buildings, where the leaders make all the important decisions."

"Okay." I sat down on the floor next to him. "Is Anna okay? You didn't tell me she had an infection."

Andy shrugged. "She gets sick all the time. The doctor gave her a prescription."

"Your mom didn't want me to go in her room. She said I'd give her germs, even though Anna's already sick."

"Mom's being extra careful. She won't let me go near Anna unless I use hand sanitizer first. She says it's important for Anna to be germ-free right now."

"Germ-free?" I waited for Andy to say something about the surgery, finally.

Instead, he just shrugged and said, "Well, something like that." Then he pulled out his notebook and opened it to the Zeraclop City diagram, like he was sweeping Anna out of his mind. But Zeraclop wasn't anything without Anna.

"Hey, do you want to work on the government buildings or the neighborhood?" Andy asked.

"I'll do the government buildings. Do you have any glitter?"

"Glitter?" Andy frowned. "There's serious stuff going on in those buildings. That's where they talk about their undercover spies—the Z.I.A. Remember?"

"I know. I was thinking if we're covering them with black construction paper, they'll look nicer with a little glitter. Like maybe gold or silver?"

Andy stared down at his notebook and didn't answer me for a while.

"Well? Don't you have some glitter?"

Andy shook his head. "At least you didn't ask for *pink* glitter."

I put down my scissors and looked up at him. "What do you mean by that?"

"Nothing."

We worked in silence for a while. I covered the buildings with ordinary black paper, while Andy began the layout of the town.

"Pink glitter is something *Madison Poplin* would want on her buildings," Andy said a few minutes later.

"So?" I said as I taped paper to the last box. "What does that have to do with me?"

"Well, if Madison likes pink glitter, you probably like it, too."

I stopped taping and looked Andy straight in the eye. "I never said anything about pink glitter. Besides, what do you have against Madison?"

Andy gave me one of those you-really-have-to-ask-me-that? looks.

"She's nice," I told him.

"Anna never liked her."

"That's not true! Anna didn't know her. I didn't know her, either, before this year."

"I just don't get why you now want to hang out with stuck-up girls like Madison, that's all."

I dropped the box on the floor. "Madison is not stuck-up."

"She's a pageant girl. Someone who wins contests by looking pretty. What do you care about that?"

"I don't."

"Then why are you hanging out with her?"

"I am *not* hanging out with her," I said, and my voice came out louder than I planned.

"And I've been wondering," Andy said as he stared at my feet. "Why are you still wearing two different shoes? I thought it was an accident on the first day of school."

I glanced at my shoes. "It was."

"Is it an accident every single day, then?"

"No. Now it's on purpose."

Andy rolled his eyes. "I don't get it."

I sighed. "It's not something I can explain." I looked him straight in the eye. "By the way, I know all about the surgery. So I'm not looking for another best friend, if that's what you think."

Andy pushed his glasses up on his nose. "What are you talking about?"

"The surgery. Anna's brain surgery! She's going to get better, and when she wakes up after it, she'll hear about all the extraordinary things I've done."

"All the things you've done?"

"Yeah. Like joining Girl Scouts and cutting my hair and taking skating lessons, like I told her I would. Plus, I'm going to be top in the class for the reading contest."

Andy snorted.

"It's true," I said. "Anna's going to be so proud of me."

Andy paused. "But, the surgery's just for her seizures. You know that, right?"

"Well, sure. That's what Mom told me. But it's brain surgery. *Brain* surgery. The doctors don't know what might happen until they operate."

Andy was shaking his head. "Mom and Dad say it's impossible for Anna to be normal again. She has permanent brain damage, Pansy."

"How do they know what's permanent? They said she wasn't going to walk again, didn't they?"

Andy nodded.

"See? They don't know what they're talking about. I know it's going to happen. And you've heard her talk in your dreams, too."

"I know," Andy said quietly. Silence filled the room. Andy stared at the notebook for a minute. Finally he said, "Look at this. There's a wall with a drawbridge surrounding the government complex. I was thinking we could cut up some of those Styrofoam trays for the wall, and then we could use real water for the moat."

I smiled. "We could use blue-green food coloring so it will look like real water, and we could line the bottom and embankments with stones."

"I think I can figure out a way to make the drawbridge open and close. I have some wires and string. And I'll just cut the box a little, like this." Andy took his pencil and outlined a rectangle on the box. Then he opened his desk drawer and pulled out a bottle of silver glitter. "We could put glitter in the water, if you want. It can be magic Zeras, to protect the government palace."

"Cool," I said, knowing Anna would agree.

## CHAPTER TWELVE

# Nine Weeks, Six Days

Pansy, are you ready?" Mom called from downstairs on Saturday morning.

"Just a minute!" I called back. This time I was prepared. I wore tights under my leggings and I had a long-sleeve shirt underneath my sweater. I threw an extra pair of gloves and socks into my bag along with earmuffs and ran down the steps.

"Are you excited?" Mom said as we drove to the Ice Palace.

Excited wasn't the word I'd use. This was something I *had* to do, like cleaning the toilets if I pulled that particular slip from the Jobs Jar Mom had sitting on the counter. "I've been waiting to take lessons forever," I finally told her.

"You know, I was just saying to your father the other night that I've never seen you so determined about anything before." Mom smiled at me in the rearview mirror. "You've set your mind on learning to skate, and that's exactly what you've done."

"Well, I wouldn't say that *exactly*. I haven't even put ice skates on yet."

"But you've been practicing on Rollerblades. Honestly, with as many times as you've fallen, we're surprised you stuck with it."

I frowned, thinking about all the times I'd already crashed, and I hadn't even stepped onto the ice yet. "I'm not too good at sports, I guess," I said in a lowered voice.

Mom shook her head. "No, that's not what I'm saying at all. We're so proud of you for sticking with it, even though it hasn't been easy. I bet ice-skating will be totally different. You'll probably take off like you've been skating all your life."

Ha ha, that was a good one. I'd already tried ice-skating, so I knew I wouldn't take off like I was born on skates. But I put on a smile as I got out of the car, pretending like I was looking forward to the whole thing, even though my insides were churning like ingredients in a mixer.

A few minutes later, I was standing at the entrance to the rink, my legs wobbly. Part of the ice was reserved for freestyle practice. Lots of little girls in short skirts flew around doing leaps and spins. And instead of putting the

Beginners' class at the front of the rink, which would make logical sense, they put it at the opposite end. Which meant I had to somehow make it across the entire length of ice. I'd be exhausted before my lesson even started.

"Go on, Pansy," my mom said. "Your teacher's waiting for you."

I stopped watching the highfliers, put my hand on the side rail, and pulled myself over to the coned-off area where my instructor stood, not once taking my hands off the bar. My ankles turned out to the sides the same way they had the last time I'd tried this crazy sport. This was nothing like Rollerblades, where you had nice solid wheels to balance on.

Why couldn't Anna have chosen something easy and less dangerous to do, like learning to meditate?

When I finally made it over to my class, the instructor, Trina, checked off our names on a list. I counted seven others, all girls except for one boy around six who was already skating better than I'd ever hope to. Most of the kids looked younger than me, and one little girl wore a pink tutu like you'd wear for dance class.

"Welcome to Beginners' Class!" Trina greeted us. "How many of you have been on skates before?"

A couple of kids raised their hands. I put up mine, too, still holding on to the rail with my left hand.

"Well, it's really quite simple. All you have to do is hold your arms out to the side and begin with small steps, picking up one foot after the other. Like this." Trina demonstrated.

Baby steps. Looked simple enough to me.

"All right, everyone face me." Trina turned toward the group. Holding her arms out to the side, she glided backward, motioning for us to follow. "And, begin!"

That's when I remembered why I spent so much time sitting on the ice during my last lesson. Following someone meant letting go of the rail. I held my arms out like Trina, picking up one foot, then the other. But instead of standing up nice and steady like my instructor did, my ankles wobbled with each step and my arms waved about in a crazy attempt to hold on to my balance.

"Great! You're doing great!" Trina coached us as we made our way across the ice.

I was halfway there. I silently congratulated myself when the second person went down and I was still standing. Must have been all that roller-blading practice. If I could make it all the way to Andy's on Rollerblades without falling, surely I could make it from one side of the ice to the other. I held my head up high and squared my shoulders with new confidence.

Next thing I knew, I was sitting on the ice. Yowch! It happened so quickly I'm not sure what made me lose my balance. All I knew was that it wasn't an easy or a graceful fall. And soon I realized something else: ice is colder than concrete and much more slippery—which means once you're down, it's hard to get back up.

I tried the method I used for getting back up on Roller-blades: I leaned forward, pushing off the ice with one hand while I tried to get to my feet. Unfortunately, it wasn't as easy as it sounded. If only the ice wasn't quite so slippery! My hand slid forward. *Splat.* I was down again.

I looked over at my instructor who was still spouting out things like, "Come on, you can do it!"

I crawled on my hands and knees until she finally came over and helped me to my feet. Or should I say, my blades.

Trina clapped once everyone was safely on the other side. "Guess now would be a good time to teach you the proper way to get up from a fall," she said with a giggle.

There was actually a trick to it. Bend down on one knee, put one foot in front of you, and push off the bent knee until you're standing up. It took a while to figure it out, but by the end of the session I'd mastered one very important thing: how to get up once I was down.

During the last few minutes of class, Trina put up cones and asked us to "slalom" in and out without knocking the cones down. She was dreaming if she thought I'd try anything like that. Just because I'd figured out how to get up from a fall didn't mean I needed to practice that skill any more than necessary.

After the lesson and once I was safely back off the ice, I collapsed on the nearest bench. I pulled off my earmuffs, the extra pair of gloves, and my heavy jacket. Wow, I was actually beginning to sweat. That must have been a sign I was working hard.

"You looked good out there," Mom said as she sat down next to me.

I stopped unlacing my skates and looked up at her. *Good?* I knew that was a lie and gave her a look.

"What?" Mom said. "I'm impressed. That roller-blading has really paid off. You looked much more confident than you did the last time."

I leaned over to pull off my skates. "Ice-skating is nothing like roller-blading."

"Well, all that skating couldn't have hurt." Mom picked up my skates and carried them over to the counter. "Did you have fun?"

I shrugged. Slipping on the ice and landing on your butt was not exactly what I'd call fun. "It was okay."

"You're coming back next week, right?" Mom said, and that's when I knew for sure that I hadn't looked confident at all.

"Don't worry, Mom. I said I'd learn to skate, and that's what I'm going to do."

Mom smiled. When we got to the parking lot, she held open the car door for me to lower my aching body onto the seat. "I'm glad you are going to stick with it. Now, how about we stop off at Yogo on the way home? I've been dying to try the salted caramel."

I smiled for the first time since we entered the rink. I'd been hoping ice-skating would come easier this time around. It hadn't, really. But I'd learned to stand up on Rollerblades, so I could learn to stand up on ice skates. Even if I broke a leg or two trying.

## CHAPTER THIRTEEN

# Seven Weeks, Four Days

I filled up the next two weeks with skating, reading, and studying. Every time Andy asked me to come over, I told him I was busy. I said I was really sorry, that I wanted to work on Zeraclop City, but that I had things I needed to do. He usually just shrugged and looked away from me. After the third time, he quit asking.

There was a space between us that hadn't been there before. We weren't arguing, and Andy didn't bring up Madison Poplin or my mismatched shoes again. But we weren't talking about Anna, either, and neither one of us said another word about the upcoming surgery.

"Anna's finally over her infection," Mom told me at breakfast. "I spoke to Mrs. Liddell last night, and she said it would be fine if you stopped by to see her one day after school this week."

"Great," I said, slurping down the rest of my cereal. "I'll go this afternoon."

When I stopped at the Liddells' after school, Anna was resting in her room. I sat on the bed and finally told her all about my goals.

"I've only had three skating lessons," I said, "but I can already baby step all the way to the other side of the rink without falling. Can you believe it?"

Anna looked up at me, her big blue eyes sparkling and clear. She looked a lot better than she had the last time I'd seen her. She was making sounds the whole time I talked to her. It sounded a little bit like "yay," except she stretched the word out, almost as though she were singing. Then she smiled out of half her mouth the way she always did now.

She was also spinning around Bright Stars, her favorite toy. It was a toy you'd buy for babies, with bright colors and lights. When you pushed the top, the stars would light up and spin.

"I'm learning forward swizzles, too," I told her. "Do you remember doing them in your lessons?"

Anna didn't stop spinning the toy. But her sound switched to something like "uh-huh." She kept sing-songing the word while I talked, but somehow I knew she was listening.

"They're not as hard as I thought. You just have to bend your knees and lean on your inside edges, but you have to be careful you don't lean too far. Or else you might fall flat on your face."

The sound switched back to "yay." Was she cheering because I might fall? Or maybe she was making a joke.

"And guess what else? Miss Quetzel posted the reading scores yesterday, and I'm in second place, right behind Daniel!"

All of a sudden Anna let out a squeal, and it was high-pitched enough that I had to cover my ears.

"I know," I said. "It's really great. You want to know my trick?"

Anna kept her eyes on the toy.

"Okay, I know I don't need a trick to win. I just need to do a lot of reading. But there's no rule that says you can't read picture books along with novels, and it's a really easy way to rack up points. The books are pretty good, too."

Anna grew quieter, making only humming sounds.

"I'm going to do it," I said. "I'm going to win the contest, just the way you wanted to last year. Oh, and tomorrow I'm going to Madison's to work on our cooking badge for Girl Scouts."

Suddenly, Anna stopped making noises. She dropped her toy to the ground. I picked it up and handed it to her. Was she upset that I was going to Madison's house? Or was she simply just tired?

I swallowed. I would have rather worked on the badge with Anna any day, even though neither of us knew how to bake. I thought about the time we baked brownies from a mix, and a grin spread across my face. "Hey, do you remember when my mom let us bake brownies by ourselves, and we added four cups of oil instead of one-fourth cup?" I giggled.

Anna looked up at me and smiled.

"But Madison says her mom lets her bake all the time. And don't worry," I told her before I left the room. "Madison is nice, but I already have a best friend."

\*\*\*

"We're going to make oatmeal chocolate chip cookies for tomorrow's meeting," Madison said as I followed her up the steps of a large white house with black shutters. Her mother had picked both of us up from school so we could work on our Girl Scout badge together. "We're making them from scratch."

I guessed scratch meant that we weren't using a mix, which sounded even more risky.

"All right, girls," Mrs. Poplin said as we entered the kitchen. "I know you're trying to earn a badge, so I'll leave you to it. If you need any help, I'll be upstairs."

"Thanks, Mom," Madison said. "We'll call you when we're ready for a taste test."

Mrs. Poplin smiled and left the room. She was trusting us alone in the kitchen, so I took it as a good sign that Madison knew what she was doing.

I sat down at the table while Madison searched for a cookbook. I wasn't someone who usually noticed kitchens, but this was the best one I'd ever seen. Bright and sunny with yellow walls, white cabinets with glass fronts, and shiny tile counters. Mom was always complaining about our kitchen. She would have loved a clean, beautiful one like this.

I watched as Madison pulled out the ingredients, measuring cups, and baking pans and piled them onto the wooden kitchen island. "You ready?" she asked.

I nodded. My stomach tightened as I got up to join her. What if I messed up everything? I could imagine Hannah's face as she bit into one of our cookies at the meeting. She'd yell, "EWWWW! This is the most disgusting thing I've ever tasted!" Then she'd spit the cookie right out into her napkin.

Madison read ingredients from the cookbook. I tried to stop picturing all of the Girl Scouts making faces and falling out of their chairs as they ate our horrible cookies.

"Slow down," I said to Madison, "or this could turn out to be a total flop."

Madison giggled. "These are super easy! I make them by myself all the time."

"You don't always have *me* as a helper."

"Don't worry, Pansy. I promise, they'll turn out perfect."

I wasn't so sure about that. I made Madison repeat everything twice, and then I double-checked my measurements before dumping anything into the mixing bowl. Luckily, Madison was telling the truth. The first lesson I learned was that a cook needs to be organized. She had all the exact measuring cups and spoons lined up in a row. She knew all about using a sifter to blend the flour, how to grease the pan so the cookies wouldn't stick, and she even knew how to crack eggs without dropping in the shells.

By the time the smell of fresh-baked cookies filled the room, my stomach was no longer in knots. Baking cookies turned out to be a whole lot easier than I thought—and much easier than learning forward swizzles.

"You want to see my room before the timer goes off?" Madison asked while the first batch was cooling on racks.

"Sure!" I jumped up to follow her. I noticed the kitchen wasn't the only room that looked like it belonged in one of those magazines you find in the dentist's office. Everything was neatly decorated; even the hallway had photos arranged in matching frames.

"Is this you?" I stopped in the stairwell and pointed to a photo of a little girl, her hair in curls, a crown on top of her head.

"Yeah," Madison said. "My first beauty pageant."

"But you're just a little kid!"

"I was three-and-a-half."

That sounded nuts to me. I kept wondering what it would be like to be a three-year-old on stage in front of judges and tons of other people when Madison said, "Come on!"

I followed her to her room and entered a world of pink. Pink canopy bed, pink rug on the floor, pink lamp, pink knobs on the dresser drawers, pink curtains, pink frames for pictures. The only things that weren't pink were the white walls and furniture.

I liked the color pink all right, but all that pink made me a little dizzy.

"Let me guess," I said. "Pink's your favorite color."

Madison nodded. "Mom went a little overboard. She did all the decorating herself."

"Oh." Luckily Mom let me decorate my own room. It was a mixture of colors—pinks, purples, blues, and yellows. Posters of animals and photos of friends stuck to the light blue walls with putty. Even my furniture was a mix from the thrift shop—a white dresser with different colored knobs and an old brown desk that people had carved their initials in. "Did she decorate the whole house?"

Madison shook her head. "Are you kidding? Mom interviewed five designers before she picked someone. She likes everything to look nice."

"I can tell. Your house is so pretty!"

"Thanks." Madison sat down on her bed.

I studied a shelf full of ribbons and trophies. "Is it fun, dressing up and entering all those beauty contests?"

Madison shrugged. "Mostly, it's kind of boring. There's a lot of waiting around, and you have to smile even when you don't feel like it. But Mom thinks pageants are the most fun thing in the world."

"Well, you must be good at it. Looks like you've won a lot of contests."

"Anyone could do it," Madison said. "All you have to do is dress up and try to look pretty."

I wasn't so sure about that. You couldn't just try to look pretty—you had to actually *be* pretty! "Well, you have to be talented, too. Don't you have to sing or dance or something?"

"Sure. I take voice, dancing, and piano lessons. But that's not why I win pageants."

I didn't know what to say about that. It sounded like Madison had just said she thought she was the prettiest girl in the world, but she didn't say it in a bragging way. Which struck me as kind of weird.

"I'm quitting when I turn thirteen," Madison said. "Pageants, not piano, I mean."

"Will your mom let you?"

"She can't tell me what to do forever. Hey, there's the timer!" Madison jumped up from the bed and raced back downstairs.

A few minutes later, we sat at the kitchen table, ready to test our oatmeal chocolate chip cookies.

"You ready?" Madison asked, holding up a cookie.

"On the count of three," I said. "One, two, three!"

We both bit into our cookies. Delicious! Awesome! Super amazing! My cookie was crunchy and melty all at the same time.

Madison's mom popped into the kitchen for a sample. "Perfect," she declared after taking a bite. "These cookies could win a contest."

"Thanks, Mom," Madison said with a grin.

The phone rang, and Mrs. Poplin disappeared again.

"You really do know how to bake cookies, Madison." I said.

"Not just me." Madison gulped down some milk. "Us. *We* know how to bake cookies."

I grinned. "We're definitely going to earn a badge for this."

Madison put two more cookies on each of our plates. "If we don't eat them all before the meeting!"

I giggled and munched away happily.

"One thing about being in pageants," Madison said as we were cleaning up the kitchen a little later, "is it keeps you busy. Sometimes too busy for friends."

"Really? But you have tons of friends."

"At school, maybe. I've never had a best friend, though."

I was shocked. "What about Emma?"

Madison shrugged. "We're good friends. But whenever she comes over, all she wants to do is talk about clothes and hair and pageant stuff. It gets pretty boring, actually."

"Oh. What about Hannah, then?"

"Hannah?" Madison shook her head. "I could never be best friends with Hannah."

"Why not?" I asked. Even though I knew why I didn't like Hannah, I wanted to know if Madison felt the same way.

"I mean, I've known Hannah since kindergarten. Our moms went to high school together. She's okay, but she always copies everything I do. And she's a big bragger, which really gets on my nerves."

"I don't think she likes me at all."

"Don't worry about that," Madison said. "She doesn't like a lot of people. The only reason I let her hang around with me is because our moms are friends. Plus, I feel a little sorry for her. Did you know her dad left a few years ago, and she doesn't even know where he is?"

I shook my head. "That's terrible," I said, wondering what it would be like if Dad walked out of the house and never came back. It wasn't even something I could imagine. It seemed like everyone had secrets—not just me—though I wasn't sure why that would make Hannah act so stuck-up. Did it make her feel better about her dad leaving when she put other people down? It didn't make sense to me.

Madison said, "Anyway, she's a lot different from you. She's always worrying about what people think, and you don't care at all."

"I don't?"

"Of course not. You cut your own hair, and look at your shoes!" Madison giggled. "Plus, you say what's on your mind."

"Is that a good thing or a bad thing?"

"It's great! I wish I could be more like you."

I felt my cheeks heat up. "Thanks," was all I could say. We were silent for a moment while sloshing around the soap suds in the kitchen sink.

"So . . . I've been meaning to ask you," Madison said quietly. "What was it like? When you saw Anna for the first time, after she got sick?"

My stomach clenched. Where had that come from? Here we were, talking about Emma and Hannah, and now Madison wanted to switch the subject to Anna?

"It must have been really . . . hard," Madison said when I didn't answer her.

I nodded as I stared down at my best friends necklace. How could I tell Madison what it felt like to see my best friend in a hospital bed, a blank look in her eyes when she used to be so full of life? How could I tell her what it felt like to lose your best friend—your other half?

"When I saw her at the park this summer, I couldn't believe it," Madison said. "It's so sad! It's almost like she died."

I shook my head and looked up at her. "No, she's still right here. She knows what's going on, even if she doesn't show it. Besides, she's not finished healing."

"What do you mean?" Madison asked me. "My parents said there's no cure for brain damage."

"Not yet."

I poured the water out of the mixing bowl and set it on the counter. Hard. Then I rinsed the last measuring cup and stuck it in the dishwasher. I glanced at the clock. "I better wait for my parents out front. They're picking me up at five, and they might not remember which house is yours."

"Okay," Madison said, drying her hands on a towel.

I looked around the kitchen, which was mostly cleaned up. "Sorry I have to leave," I told her. "Mom doesn't like to wait."

"It's all right. We're almost finished anyway," Madison said, following me out the door. "I'm sorry—I didn't mean anything about Anna—"

"I know."

Then she spoke so softly, I couldn't tell if she was speaking to me or to herself. "It's just—I think Anna is lucky to have you as a best friend."

## CHAPTER FOURTEEN

# Six Weeks, Four Days

I've printed out the latest Independent Reader scores," Miss Quetzel announced as she posted the print-out on the bulletin board. "Looks like quite a few of you have earned enough for popsicles in the room at lunch this Friday. So, now's a good time to take a few minutes so that you can spend your money."

I felt a tap on my shoulder while Miss Quetzel was calling students to collect their rewards.

"Are you going to use your bucks on popsicles?" Madison asked me.

I nodded. "Are you?"

"Of course!" Madison grinned at me. "We'll have so much fun!"

I glanced over at Andy. "How about you?" I asked him. "Do you want to stay in the room on Friday with us and have popsicles?"

Andy shrugged. I turned around and started talking to Madison, and a few minutes later, Andy got up to spend his money on a homework pass. Maybe he hadn't earned enough points for the popsicles. Or was it that he didn't want to stay in the room since I was talking to Madison? Whatever the reason, he didn't say anything more about it. He just stuck the homework pass in his folder and turned back around in his seat instead of joining our conversation.

"Now," Miss Quetzel said once she'd finished with the Reading Bucks, "it's time for social studies. Today we're going to begin group projects on the Civil War. I've decided to let you choose your own group members—no more than four to a group."

An excited buzz filled the room. Miss Quetzel had never let us choose our own groups before. I'd work with Andy, of course, but before I could turn to him Madison leaned forward and said, "Come on, Pansy! Join our group. This is going to be awesome!"

I glanced at Andy. He shrugged and stared down at his desk.

"Um, what about Andy?" I asked Madison.

She looked over at Emma and Hannah, who were making their way toward us.

"No offense, Andy," she said, "but our group is girls only."

"No problem," Andy said. But from the look on his face, I could tell it hurt his feelings. He picked up his notebook and walked across the room where some boys were looking for team members. I knew he'd find someone else to work with, but I didn't like the way he'd walked away without even smiling at me.

Madison, however, gave me a wide smile as I pulled my chair up to her desk. I felt my lips curving up at the corners, even though I hadn't meant to smile back. I wanted to work with Andy, but working with Madison would be fun, too.

"We're going to do the best job in the class," Madison said once we'd gathered around her desk. She folded her arms in front of her. "I think we should dress up when we give our oral reports."

"I call Mrs. Lincoln!" Hannah said.

"I think Madison should be Mary Todd Lincoln," Emma said. "She has this beautiful pageant gown that looks just like something Mrs. Lincoln would wear."

"That's true," Madison said. "Besides, I read a biography about Lincoln last year, so I know all about her."

Hannah crossed her arms in front of her chest and pouted.

"I'll be Clara Barton," Emma said. "She was a famous nurse during the Civil War."

"I'll be Abraham Lincoln," I said. "I have a big black hat at home just like his."

"You'll need a beard, too," Hannah said.

"I can make one," I said. "Unless you want to be Abraham Lincoln?"

Hannah shook her head. "I'm sure there's some other famous ladies. I'm not dressing up as a boy."

Emma giggled. "Pansy doesn't mind."

"I didn't say that exactly," I said. "But *someone* has to be Abraham Lincoln. Since we're studying the war and all."

"Thanks, Pansy," Madison said. "I knew you were going to be a great team member!" And she reached over and squeezed my hand.

Hannah made a face.

"Girls," Miss Quetzel said, walking over to us, "You're supposed to divide up the research material and get started. After you finish all the research, then you can worry about the presentation part."

"Okay, Miss Quetzel," Madison said. For the next thirty minutes, we argued about who was going to do what and how we were going to do it. Or mostly the other girls argued, and I sat there and watched.

"It doesn't matter to me which part I do," I said when Miss Quetzel gave us the five-minute warning. "Just tell me and I'll start on it tonight."

"I've got an idea," Emma suggested. "Why don't we put all the assignments in a bag and everyone can pull one out?"

"Sounds like a plan." Madison tore off pieces of notebook paper. Each of us had an assignment in our hand just as Miss Quetzel called time. I'd ended up with Abraham Lincoln, and I really didn't mind. Hannah took one look at hers and made a grumpy face before returning to her seat.

"See you at lunch," Madison said as I pulled my chair back to the front row.

***

Andy was smiling when he came back to his seat after social studies.

"Did you get a good group?" I asked him.

"The best," Andy said. "I'm working with Luke, Bryce, and Daniel."

"Daniel? Did you get him to say anything?"

"Sure," Andy said. "He's really nice."

"That's great," I said, and I meant it. I was glad Andy had found a group to work with. Just because Daniel was standing between me and the reading trophy didn't mean he wouldn't make a good group partner for Andy.

"Hey, Andy," Emma said as we walked up to the girls at their regular spot in the cafeteria. I sat down next to Madison, and Andy sat down across from me. "Do you think Anna can come to the autumn party next week?"

My mouth dropped open, but I closed it quickly, not wanting anyone to notice. Invite Anna to the class party? What a crazy idea!

"My mom's the room mom this year," Emma continued, "and she wants to invite her."

I looked over at Andy. How did he feel about having Anna in the classroom, everyone gathering around her, whispering and staring? Or even worse, talking to her like she's a baby? I mean, sure, a lot of kids had already seen Anna, out at the park or in the grocery store or at church. But to have her in our classroom where she used to be one of the top students?

It would be worse than awful.

Andy scooped up a spoonful of Spaghetti-O's without looking at Emma. "Anna won't be able to make it."

"It's because of the seizures," I said quickly. "Anna's been having really bad seizures. And Mrs. Liddell probably doesn't want to bring her somewhere that's noisy and crowded because it can set off the seizures—"

"It doesn't have anything to do with that," Andy cut in. "She doesn't go to this school anymore, and she can't come to the party, that's all."

"Oh," Emma said, sounding disappointed. "That's too bad."

"Does it hurt to have seizures?" Madison asked. "What happens when she has one?"

"It's like a fainting spell," I told her. "She falls down and her eyes roll back in her head—"

"It's no big deal," Andy said, shooting me a dirty look. "She takes medicine for it. Can we talk about something else?"

"Sorry," Madison said. "I was hoping we'd see Anna at the party."

"Me too," Emma said.

Andy shrugged and shoveled large spoonfuls of Spaghetti-O's into his mouth, one after another.

Madison, Emma, and I glanced at each other. I could tell they were waiting for me to speak, but what was I supposed to say?

Madison came to the rescue. "What kind of presentation is your group doing for social studies, Andy?" she asked.

A smile spread slowly across his face. "It's going to be really cool. We're doing a game show, with prizes and everything! What are you guys doing?"

"Can't tell you," Madison said quickly, then looked at the rest of us and put her finger to her lips.

"Why not?"

"It's a secret," Hannah said.

"It's going to be awesome!" Emma said.

I looked around at the other girls. "*If* we get the work done."

Andy turned to me. "Pansy will eventually tell me."

"No, she won't." Madison winked at me. "She's good at keeping secrets, right?"

I nodded. "Sorry, Andy. You'll have to wait and see."

"Who came up with the idea for a game show?" Hannah asked. "I bet it was Daniel."

"Actually, it was my idea," Andy said.

"Andy has great ideas—" I started to say, but Hannah interrupted.

"So, why'd you pick Daniel for your group, anyway? He's a pretty weird kid," Hannah said. "I've never heard him say a word."

"He only talks to people who know how to listen," Andy said. "Besides, he doesn't waste time arguing."

Emma giggled, then clapped a hand over her mouth when Hannah glared at her.

"You know what? I think I'll go sit with him right now." Andy picked up his tray and headed to the end of the table to sit next to Daniel before I could stop him.

"What did you do that for?" I asked Hannah. "Why were you so rude to him?"

Hannah shrugged. "Who wants to sit with a boy at lunch anyway?"

Madison ran her fingers through her hair. "I kind of like sitting with him."

"Me too," I said quietly.

As I sat there half-listening to the conversations around me, I replayed in my mind what had happened a few minutes earlier. I pictured Andy's face when I'd mentioned Anna's seizures. Had I embarrassed him when I talked about Anna?

I glanced over at Andy where he sat with Daniel and some other boys. I knew the truth about why Andy had moved to a new lunchtime spot, but I wasn't sure what to do about it.

Hannah wasn't the only reason Andy had left the table.

## CHAPTER FIFTEEN

# Five Weeks, Four Days

The autumn party turned out to have a theme: life in the US during the 1800s. Miss Quetzel was all about making things educational. After we made cornbread from a mix and butter that we had to shake in jars just like in the nineteenth century, we pushed the chairs back for a big square dance.

"Since we're trying to be authentic here," Miss Quetzel said as she held up a paper bag, "the dance will be boy-girl."

Laughter and groans mixed together. All I could think was, *If I end up with Zach Turansky, I will just die.*

When it was my turn, I closed my eyes tight, crossed my fingers, and squinched up my toes as I reached in the bag. *Please let it be Andy,* I said over and over in my head. And when

I opened the slip of paper and saw Daniel's name, I let out a big breath. It was tons better than Zach, but did I really want to dance with Nose-in-a-Book Daniel, the boy who kept Anna—and me—from being number one in the reading contest?

Miss Quetzel, however, didn't mind dancing with Daniel at all. She jumped to her feet and demonstrated all the steps, sashaying with her partner before she turned on the music and let us give it a try. It ended up being a lot of fun. Daniel didn't have sweaty hands, and he didn't stomp on my feet on purpose, like a lot of the other boys would have. He smiled at me while we do-si-doed and laughed when he messed up. Turns out he was much nicer than I'd thought.

After the square dance, we did some paper weaving and made stovetop hats, just like President Lincoln wore. Then we ate the cornbread and butter and drank hot cider.

"Want to come over to work on Zeraclop today?" Andy asked while we ate our snack. I looked up at him. It was the first time he'd asked in a while, and more than anything I wanted to say yes. But then I remembered all the extra work I had now that we'd started the social studies project, on top of all the other extraordinary things I had to stay on top of.

I shook my head. "I can't," I told him. "I have to work on the research for the project."

"Oh, come on," Andy said. "Our group got most of ours done in class."

"Well, Madison has special plans for our project, so that means a lot of homework," I said. Madison had this idea that we had to actually write a skit instead of just dress up and read our reports. "Sorry," I told Andy. "I wish I could."

"Whatever." Andy turned away from me, but not before I saw disappointment flash in his eyes. My stomach sloshed, and for a second I almost said, "It's all right, I can put off my homework for one day."

Then I remembered how I'd moved up to second place in the reading contest, right behind Daniel. Any day now, I'd fly right past him. And I couldn't skip afternoon roller-blading practice. I was finally getting the hang of it, but missing a practice could mean a rough time on the ice at Saturday morning's class.

I had a little over a month until Anna's surgery to prove I was extraordinary. Zeraclop would have to wait.

*** 

I noticed the shoes right away. Madison showed up at school with one pink and one lavender, both the same style. Emma wore a brown shoe with a strap across her ankle and a white tennis shoe with laces.

"So, what do you think?" Madison said as we headed toward the blacktop at recess the next day. She kicked her pink foot in the air.

"Well . . ." I hesitated a minute. Her shoes were the same shade of pink and lavender as the flowers on her skirt. "Your shoes match your outfit. It looks like you did it on purpose."

"Of course I did it on purpose. I had to sneak my lavender shoe in my backpack and change in the bathroom before class. Mom wouldn't have liked it, even if I am color-coordinated."

"My mom didn't notice," Emma said. "I knew she wouldn't. Things are very hectic around our house in the mornings."

"Why didn't you tell me you were going to wear different shoes today?" Hannah asked as she ran to keep up with us. "I have two different boots that would look so cool together."

"It just sort of happened," Madison said. "Actually, Emma and I were talking about it on the way home yesterday. I didn't know she was actually going to do it, though."

"And I didn't know *she* was going to do it!" Emma said with a giggle.

Hannah frowned. "I wish you had told me about it."

"It's not like we planned it," Madison said. "Pansy's the one who started it. But I've gotten so many compliments today! I bet a lot more girls in our class will wear mismatched shoes to school tomorrow."

"Just think," Emma said to me. "It was all your idea! What made you wear two different shoes on the first day of school anyway?"

"Well, the truth is . . . I did it by accident."

"By accident?" Hannah repeated.

"Yup. I was rushing around, and I was worried about my haircut—"

"Which is still a little crooked," Hannah said.

Both girls turned to stare at Hannah.

"You are so rude," Madison said to her.

"What?" Hannah said. "I'm only being honest."

"It's no big deal," I told them. "Hannah's right. My haircut's all lopsided. And on the first day of school, I was busy thinking about how I looked when it was time to find my shoes."

"So, why'd you keep wearing two different pairs each day then?" Emma asked.

I shrugged. "Once I started, it was hard to stop."

"I still think they look funny," Hannah said, staring down at my feet.

Madison turned on Hannah. "If you think Pansy looks funny, then you must think the same thing about us."

"No," Hannah said quickly. "Your shoes look great, Madison!"

Madison held her chin up high. "If you don't like Pansy's hair and if you don't like Pansy's shoes, then maybe you need to find someone else to hang out with."

Hannah shook her head and looked over at me. "No, I mean, I like *you*, Pansy—"

"Well, you sure don't act like it," Madison said. "And if you want to be friends with us, then you have to be nice to Pansy, too."

"Okay, sure. I'm sorry, Pansy," she said. She didn't exactly sound like she meant it, but who cares? Madison had stuck up for me, and that's what mattered.

Madison put one arm around me and one around Emma. I couldn't help grinning. "Come on, let's go to the swings!" she said, and we headed to the playground, Hannah trailing behind.

## CHAPTER SIXTEEN

# Three Weeks, Four Days

It was finally time for our Civil War presentations. After weeks of research, skit-writing, rehearsing, and listening to Hannah whine, I was ready for the project to be over. I hurried into the classroom the morning of the presentations and carefully hung the bag with my costume in it on a coat hook on the back wall.

"Pansy!" Madison called to me from where she stood by the bulletin board. "Come look!"

A crowd gathered around the latest Independent Reader postings, and I knew from Madison's face that it had to be good news. As soon as I walked over, she threw her arm around me. "You're in *first* place!"

"Really?" I stared at the paper, and there was my name at the top of the list. I blinked to make sure I was seeing it clearly. For a moment, the thought flashed through my head that I might have earned some of those points unfairly. But before I knew it, I was surrounded by girls cheering and telling me how great it was that someone had finally beaten Daniel Walker, and I pushed the thought right out of my head.

I was number one, for the first time in my life!

As I stood there listening to the girls congratulating me, I thought back to last fall, when Anna told me she wanted to win the reading contest. "I'm going to earn more points than anyone!" she had said as we stood in the library looking for books to check out. She had looked over at me and added, "I've got an even better idea! Let's both earn the most points. Then we can share the trophy!"

I'd giggled at the idea of sharing the trophy. Besides, racing through a bunch of books just to earn points didn't sound so exciting to me—especially not last year.

"That's okay," I had said with a grin. "I'll let you have it."

Now I couldn't wait to tell her the news. Because of Anna, I was now in first place, and we could still share that trophy!

Zach's voice broke through the chatter of congratulations. "You won't be in first place for long," he sneered. "Haven't you seen the book Daniel's been lugging around lately? It weighs about ten pounds, and it's gonna be worth tons of points. Just wait till he takes his next test, he'll blow you away."

"Like I care what *you* think." I shot him a dirty look and pushed past him to my seat. Today, I was in first place, and no one was going to change that—not even Zach Turansky.

Soon it was time for our presentations. Madison changed into a long velvet pageant dress and piled her hair up on top of her head. I changed into black pants, the black hat I made at our autumn party, and Mom's suit jacket, which was too long and hung off my shoulders.

Everyone oohed and aahed when Madison walked into the room. No one really noticed Hannah the spy in her plain black dress or Emma in her jean skirt and nurse's cap. They were too busy admiring Madison and then laughing at me.

Oh, well. It was hard to look elegant when you were dressed like Abraham Lincoln. Especially if your beard was made out of construction paper, cotton balls, and string.

Our skit began with a conversation between Mr. and Mrs. Lincoln at the supper table. "This biscuit is delicious," I said, picking up a piece of plastic bread and pretending to take a bite.

"Yes," Madison said, dabbing at her mouth with a handkerchief. "Maggie is such a wonderful cook! Now, darling, what news do you have about the war?"

"I received a report today from the generals." I reached under my plate for my report about the battles. As I leaned forward, my hat fell off my head, knocking over my plastic cup of real ice tea.

I inhaled quickly. I tried to grab my report, but it was too late. The tea had already spread across my paper, making the ink impossible to read.

Muffled giggles, coughs, and snorts filled the room.

Luckily, it was only a copy of the one I'd pasted onto our poster. "Um, it's right here." I picked up my hat and moved to where our poster was tacked to the board. I read from the poster like we had practiced, and all was going well until I heard another giggle.

My hat slipped down over my eyes and I pushed it up so I could see. I stared out at the audience. Everyone was staring at us, and they looked amused. Civil War battles weren't exactly entertaining stuff, so I knew it had to be something else—me!

I'd looked at myself in the mirror when I dressed up at home, and there wasn't anything funny about my outfit. So why did I keep hearing those scattered sounds from the classroom, sounds that told me someone was trying hard not to laugh out loud?

Was it the hat that I had to keep straightening on my head? Or was it the much-too-big suit with the rolled-up sleeves? Or maybe . . . could it be . . . gasp! Was my fly unzipped?

I tried to concentrate on reading out the facts of the war. But all I could think about was my zipper. Somehow, I had to sneak a look without making it obvious—but how?

If I looked away from the poster for a second, I'd lose my place. Then Miss Quetzel might not give me a very good grade on the presentation.

The solution popped in my head as I finished reporting on the Battle of Williamsburg. I turned from the poster and said to Madison, "Mary, dear, will you pass me another biscuit?"

More sound effects from the audience. Madison wrinkled her eyebrows like she was trying to figure out what I was doing. She handed me a biscuit so quickly I didn't have time to glance at my zipper. So I handed the biscuit back to her and said, "With butter, please?"

While Madison pretended to butter a plastic piece of bread, I stole a glance at my pants.

Whew. I let out my breath slowly. It wasn't my zipper! So what in the world was everyone laughing at?

"Some people are not being very respectful listeners," Miss Quetzel said to hush them up.

I looked over at Andy in the front row. He had his hand clamped over his mouth, like he was trying not to make a sound.

I reached for the biscuit. Madison opened her eyes wide and motioned with her head to look down. I'd already checked my pants, and I knew I was safe. I squinted back at her. She ran her hand across her chin.

I reached up to touch my beard. It was hanging halfway off my face! So that was the problem! I turned around and reached up to fix it. My foot landed on something soft. When I glanced at the floor, I noticed the pile of cotton balls around my feet.

What should I do now? Keep going with the presentation, pretending like half my beard was not scattered across the floor and all I had was a brown piece of construction paper hanging from my chin? Or stop, pick up the cotton balls, fix my beard, and then finish with the presentation?

I glanced back at Madison, hoping she'd make the call. But she just shook her head and shrugged, like she had no idea what to do.

And that's when I made a decision. A decision to save our skit. "Excuse me folks. We need to pause for a brief commercial break." I looked over at Hannah and Emma, who stood off to one side, waiting for their cue. "This commercial announcement brought to you by Hannah and Emma. Back in a moment!"

Hannah and Emma looked at each other. Then Hannah walked to the front of the room and did her best to sell for "Civil War Biscuits," straight off of Madison's plate. The other girls joined in, and while they put on a biscuit commercial, I picked up all the cotton balls, grabbed some tape from my desk, and stuck them back on my beard. Then I retied my scarf, straightened my hat, and returned to my spot just as Hannah was taking a fake bite into the biscuit and saying, "Mmm, mmm, good!"

"And now," I said, staring bravely out at my classmates, "back to your regularly scheduled program."

We finished the rest of our skit without a hitch. The class broke into applause at the end. I bowed, the others curtsied, and I found it hard to keep a smile off my face as I returned to my seat.

I, Pansy Smith, felt truly extraordinary.

***

"Great presentation, Pansy!" Andy said as we headed to the playground at recess.

"Thanks." I followed him up the monkey bars and sat next to him. "Why didn't you tell me that my beard was falling off? I looked right at you, and I could tell you were trying not to laugh."

"I motioned to you. Didn't you see me put my hand on my chin?"

I shook my head. "You covered your mouth. But you never touched your chin."

"Sure I did." Andy flipped through his notebook until he found his Zeraclop City drawings. "It's okay, though. That's what made it so funny. What made you think to stall with the commercial?"

"Well, I had to do something! Hey, since I'm finished with my research, maybe I can come over this afternoon to work on the city."

Andy looked up from his notebook. "Really? I thought you were busy with reading. And skating. And Girl Scouts."

"I can take a day off, you know."

Daniel waved up at us, and I waved back. I noticed he was holding a book, some thick one with dragons on the cover, but today he wasn't reading while wandering the playground.

"Hi, Daniel," Andy said, climbing down from the bars. "I have that notebook I was telling you about."

"Cool," Daniel said.

My mouth dropped right open as I stared at the two of them, talking and laughing. Andy had told Daniel about Zeraclop City? It was supposed to be private, between Anna, Andy, and me!

I jumped down after him. "You told Daniel about the notebook?"

Andy handed the notebook to Daniel, then looked at the ground. "Daniel likes to create cities, too. He's coming over this afternoon to work on it with me."

"Yeah, it sounds awesome." Daniel put his book down and flipped through the notebook. "Wow, you are some artist, Andy!"

"Thanks," Andy said.

"But—but that was *our* city, Andy." My voice dropped to a whisper. "We started working on it with Anna, remember?"

Andy looked over at me and shoved his hands in his pockets. "Yeah, sure. But she can't work on it with me now.

And you're always too busy. Daniel was interested, so I thought I could use his help, too." He turned to Daniel. "Come on, let's go to the field. Bryce and Luke want to see the plans, too."

I crossed my arms in front of my chest and kicked the dirt with my foot. How could Andy do something like this? He didn't ask my permission, and he certainly hadn't asked Anna's!

Daniel turned to look at me. "You coming, Pansy?"

I shook my head, my eyes watering as I watched them walk away. Andy was supposed to be my *friend*. So what if I'd been too busy over the last few weeks to help him work on the city? Zeraclop was special to me—and to Anna. Didn't that mean anything to him?

"Pansy!" I was startled out of my thoughts as a group of girls suddenly surrounded me, telling me they liked my costume and my presentation.

"It was the best in the class," Samantha Dawkins said.

"Yeah," Lisa Pierce agreed. "It wasn't boring at all."

"The commercial was so funny!" Janet Beene added.

Madison, Emma, and Hannah joined, too. "We've been looking for you, Pansy!" Madison said. "I saw Andy on the field, but he was with a bunch of boys."

"Yeah," I said. "I guess he'd rather hang out with them than me."

"That's okay," Madison said, linking her arm with mine. "You've got us to hang out with now. And that's way better than any old boy!"

## CHAPTER SEVENTEEN

# Two Weeks, Four Days

The week before Thanksgiving, I pulled out my calendar and crossed off another day, just like I had every other night since I'd found out about Anna's surgery. But the fluttering that I'd felt inside when I first heard the news had turned into something more solid, like a weight in the bottom of my stomach.

I couldn't stop thinking about it. What if something went wrong during the surgery? What if the surgeon made a mistake and instead of fixing Anna's brain caused even more damage? What if Anna got another infection, one she wasn't strong enough to fight off? What if my mom was right, and there really was no cure for brain damage?

I kept trying to toss those questions out of my head, trying to focus on reading or skating or studying, but as soon as I went to bed, there they were again, racing through my mind.

I thought about Anna, how she was always good at calming me down when I was worried about something. During our poetry unit last year, everyone had to memorize a poem and recite it in front of the entire fourth grade. Parents were invited to the event, there was a reception afterward, and awards were given out for first, second, and third place.

Anna picked a long poem that was written in the olden days, and she memorized the whole thing in a day. I picked out a short funny poem, but I knew I'd forget the words once I got up in front of all those people.

"You can do it," Anna kept telling me as we recited our poems. "Just pretend like we're on our way to school, and it's only me, you, and Andy."

I shook my head. "How can I pretend like we're walking to school when I'm standing up on stage in front of all those people? I'll forget the words, for sure."

Anna stopped in the middle of the sidewalk. "Now, close your eyes and say the poem."

So I did, and Anna burst into applause.

"How's that gonna work?" Andy asked. "You want Pansy to close her eyes while she's standing on stage?"

"Sure. There's no rule that says you have to have your eyes open, is there?"

"I don't know . . ." I said as we started walking again. "It'll look pretty weird if I have my eyes closed."

"Who cares?" Anna said. "If it keeps you from having stage fright, then it doesn't matter. You might even win the contest."

I laughed.

"It's true." Anna gave my hand a squeeze. "You did a really good job reciting that poem just now."

Anna's idea worked. I stood up on stage, closed my eyes, and pretended it was just me, Anna, and Andy on our way to school. I didn't win any awards, but I got through it, and that's what mattered.

Anna won third place. But when it was all over, she seemed more excited about me than she did about her ribbon. "You did it!" she said, throwing her arms around me as we stood near the snack table afterward. "Just like I knew you would."

No matter how worried or nervous I was, Anna always believed in me. And I knew she still did. I would never have put on skates, gone to the top of the list for Independent Reader, or joined Girl Scouts if it weren't for Anna. But now, it was my turn to be there for her. To believe that she was going to pull through this surgery, that she was going to come out of it stronger than ever before. That she was going to be Anna again and that she would be so proud of me for all I'd done. So I blocked out all those questions and concentrated on one thing only: in less than two weeks, I'd be sure to have my best friend back.

\*\*\*

My grandparents came to visit for Thanksgiving. Dad baked his special chocolate pecan pie, and Mom made her famous sweet potatoes to go with the other dishes. When Mom and Dad told my grandparents they were really proud of me for all my hard work in fifth grade, I felt myself glowing from the inside out.

"Congratulations!" Grandma gave me a warm smile. "First place in the reading contest! We knew you could do it!"

The reason I'd worked so hard was because of Anna, so I felt a little guilty that I wanted to wrap all that praise around me like a nice warm blanket. But I didn't feel too guilty. *I* was proud of myself, too . . . well, except for the first three points I'd earned for a book I read that summer. And then there was that nagging voice that appeared sometimes, the one that said, *The only reason you've earned so many points is because you read a lot of extra kiddie books. Do you really deserve to be the champion?*

"Great job, Pansy," Grandpop said with a wink. "But don't forget to leave time for fun."

"Oh, you!" Grandma said, giving Grandpop a little shoulder punch. "Of course she's having fun! Baking cookies for Girl Scouts, ice-skating at the rink, and she loves to read, don't you, Pansy?"

I nodded.

"She looks pretty happy to me," Grandma said.

"I am happy," I said. "I never thought I could do all this stuff, but it turns out I can."

Everyone laughed, then they asked all kinds of questions about Girl Scouts and skating and school.

But after supper I thought about what Grandpop said. Reading used to be fun, back when I could pick out the books I wanted instead of just choosing ones that earned the most points. I could read in a lazy way instead of rushing to get through each book. Girl Scouts with Madison could also be fun, but I was already thinking about the next badge we had to complete and worrying about that camping trip in the spring. And ice-skating is plain hard work. What's fun about having to remember to bend your knees and keep your head up, your arms out, and your ankles strong to avoid landing on your butt every time you take a step? Plus, that rink is freezing! Does anyone really like having frozen fingers and toes?

I used to enjoy just hanging around and having fun. But this year, it wasn't something I'd included on my list of goals. Anna loved to have fun. Why had I forgotten all about it?

For a minute, I almost told my parents I was going over to Anna's, like I usually did after we ate our Thanksgiving meal. Our families both ate around the same time, so afterward we'd meet up and talk about how full we were. Then we'd head outside to the swing set or hang out in the treehouse, or sometimes our families would come together to play board games together in the evening.

This was the first time we missed a Thanksgiving get-together, at least that I could remember. No one from the Liddell house called and asked us to come over, and even though I wanted to pick up the phone and invite myself over, I couldn't. Ever since Andy shared Zeraclop City with Daniel and the other boys, I felt a coolness between us that I didn't know how to fix.

## CHAPTER EIGHTEEN

# Four Days

I am so excited!" Miss Quetzel said the first day back after Thanksgiving break. "The Good Citizens party is only a few weeks away, and according to our chart," she said, turning toward the board, "we're only a few points away from earning the reward! Now, I've spoken to management at the Ice Palace, and they'll block off part of the ice for those who want lessons during our party. We'll also have the party room for snacks afterward."

The class cheered and whooped. I grinned. Everything was coming together just like I'd planned. I was finally learning to ice-skate, and no one would laugh at me during the class party. Not even Zach Turansky.

"Can we have races?" Zach asked after Miss Quetzel finished her pep talk about earning those last few points.

"Races?" Miss Quetzel frowned. "Maybe, if everyone is careful—"

The room exploded in applause. I chewed on my lip. With all my Rollerblade practice and my ice-skating lessons, maybe *I'd* join in, too. Anna would be so surprised if I entered a race . . . especially if I actually won.

\*\*\*

"Let's go sit at the other end of the table," I told Madison as we walked into the cafeteria.

Andy had been sitting with Daniel ever since we started working on our research projects, but whenever there were empty seats near them, I made sure that's where we sat. Sometimes, though, Andy didn't seem to notice. Lately, he and Daniel were talking all the time, drawing new plans for Zeraclop City, and they never asked me to join them. Right now their heads leaned toward one another as they peered over the notebook Andy, Anna, and I had started together.

I felt something boiling up inside of me, and I didn't like it at all.

When I set my tray down next to Andy, he looked up at me and blinked, like he was surprised to see me.

"I can't wait to watch Miss Quetzel skate at the party," Emma said once we were seated. "She'll probably do a special routine for us. I hope she wears a pink skating dress. I bet it'll have sequins on it and everything."

"I call first in line for lessons!" Madison said. "I've only been skating once, and I fell about ten times."

I looked at her. I couldn't picture it—pretty, graceful Madison losing her balance and falling on the ice, just like me?

"I've only been skating once, and I fell *thirty* times!" Emma said with a giggle.

Hannah didn't volunteer any information about what kind of skater she was, but if she wasn't bragging, I could bet she wasn't an expert either. I might turn out to actually be the best one in the group! Except for Anna, that is.

My stomach flipped over at the thought that she would be there, skating next to me.

"I went roller-blading with Pansy at Gateway Park," Andy said, glancing at me. "You should have seen her."

I stared back at Andy. He held my gaze a moment longer, then looked straight at Madison and said, "Did Pansy ever tell you about the time she got pulled by three dogs across the park?"

Laughter rose into the air. I felt my face heat up from my cheeks all the way to the tips of my ears. He'd promised not to say a word to anyone about that!

"It's true," Andy said. "Pansy was trying to learn how to roller-blade, and she got tangled up in their leashes. She came about this close"—I watched in horror as he held up his thumb and pointer finger—"to landing in the duck pond."

"I did *not* almost land in the duck pond," I said, but no one was listening. Emma and Madison were giggling. Hannah hee-hawed, and even Daniel let out a hoot.

I narrowed my eyes at Andy.

"Why didn't you just let go of the leashes?" Daniel asked when the laughter died down.

"Of course I let go of the leashes."

"She sure did," Andy said. "It was a spectacular fall, too."

I shot him a dirty look.

"Weren't you scared?" Madison asked me. "I would have been scared to death."

"The dogs must have been running really fast," Emma added.

"They were flying," I said. There was no point denying it now, so I made the most of it. "They were going about a hundred miles an hour!"

"Actually," Daniel said, "it couldn't have been a hundred miles an hour. Unless you were being pulled by cheetahs."

Andy laughed louder than necessary at Daniel's joke.

What was wrong with Andy? Why was he being so mean to me? First, he shared Zeraclop City when it was supposed to be private between me and Anna and him. And now, here he was, trying to get people to make fun of me after he had promised not to tell what happened that day at the park!

"It's not like you're such a great skater," I spat out toward him. "Anna's the one with all the coordination. She could skate circles around you."

A shadow passed over Andy's eyes, and he looked down at his lunch. One minute he was having a great time watching everyone laugh at me. But as soon as I mentioned Anna's name, everything changed.

"Anna wasn't only good at roller-blading," I continued, glad no one was laughing at me anymore. "She took ice-skating lessons, too. Andy wouldn't even sign up. It's obvious who got the athletic talent in the Liddell family," I said with a laugh.

No one joined in my laughter. Instead, my words had sent a hush across the table. Everyone just stared at me, like they were shocked at what I had said. I didn't get why they were shocked—Andy had told the truth about me; now I was telling the truth about him.

Andy peeled his orange peel off in a long spiral. When he spoke, his voice was so low I had to lean forward to hear him. "Why do you always do that? Why do you always bring up Anna?"

I sat back in my seat and crossed my arms in front of my chest. "I happen to like talking about Anna."

"Well, this conversation doesn't have anything to do with her."

Andy did not have the right to tell me when I could or couldn't talk about Anna. "It has everything to do with Anna," I said, running my fingers over my necklace. "Besides, I can talk about her whenever I want to. She's my best friend, you know."

Andy's eyes locked with mine. "But she's *my* twin sister," he said. Then he picked up his uneaten orange, threw it in his lunchbox, and shut the lid tight. He stood, pushed his chair in so that it banged against the table, grabbed his lunchbox, and stormed out of the cafeteria without stopping to ask permission to leave.

"Oooh, Andy's in big trouble now," Hannah said. "I sure hope Miss Quetzel doesn't take Good Citizens points away from the class for his misbehavior in the cafeteria."

"There are more important things than Good Citizens points," I snapped back at her. I wanted to run after Andy and ask him why he was so angry. Was it because I'd said Anna was more athletic than he was? Andy knew it was the truth, and he never seemed to care before. I knew he couldn't really be mad about the fact that I liked to talk about Anna . . . Was it something else, something that I hadn't said at the table? Did it have something to do with Anna's surgery? It was this Friday, only a few days away. We hadn't talked about the surgery again, not since I first told him I knew about it. But then we hadn't spent that much time together lately, except for on the way to school.

As we got closer to the big day, I found that I didn't want to talk about it at all. Just saying the words "Anna's brain surgery" gave me a funny feeling in the pit of my stomach.

Well, it didn't really matter what Andy was upset about. I couldn't go after him, not after he'd broken his promise and embarrassed me in front of everyone. Besides, if I left the cafeteria without permission, I might get blamed by my class if we lost Good Citizens points.

It was Daniel Walker, not me, who got up from the table.

"I can't believe it!" Hannah said. "They are both going to be in so much trouble."

I didn't say anything as I watched Daniel push open the door of the cafeteria, letting it swing shut behind him.

"What's going on with you two anyway?" Madison asked me.

"Don't know," I mumbled as I stared at the cafeteria doors. Even though I was still mad at Andy, I should have been the one with the guts to get up and follow him. Instead, I sat glued to my seat, unable to move.

"Andy must have been really upset to leave the cafeteria," Madison said.

"Yeah," Emma said. "I've never seen you two argue before."

I shrugged. Then I folded my arms on the table, put my head down, and shut my eyes tight. Even though the girls kept shooting questions at me, I didn't say a word to anyone for the rest of lunch period.

## CHAPTER NINETEEN

# Four Days

When Andy was sent home early, I wondered if it had anything to do with Anna's surgery. I walked alone that afternoon. I was trying to figure out how to make things right between us again, not paying attention to where I was walking, when I landed in something squashy. I stopped and looked down at my feet.

Great. Just great. This was all I needed on top of my perfectly awful day. I'd landed smack in a pile of fresh dog poop. I picked up my foot and scraped it on the grass, but the poop had already smeared on the sides of my pink shoe.

Now what? I always carried the other blue shoe with me so I could change before I got home. But what was I supposed to do with the dirty one? I couldn't stick it in my backpack. I scraped it in the grass again, but the poop had seeped into the treads on the bottom of my sole and had smushed around the sides, too.

A block from my house, I changed so I'd walk inside the house wearing a matching pair like always. But this time I had to carry a dog-pooped pink shoe between two fingers the rest of the way home. Luckily, there was a note on the kitchen table when I walked inside, saying that Mom had an emergency meeting and would be home in twenty minutes. So I used a wet paper towel to scrape off whatever I could before throwing my shoes in the washing machine.

Then I tossed in the blue shoe, to get it extra clean as well. I looked over at the pile of clothes in the laundry basket. Mom was always saying it would be nice if I helped out around the house once in a while. But for a second, I hesitated, wondering if it was okay to wash a poopy shoe with regular clothes.

Then I saw the words on the detergent bottle: GUARANTEED TO ZAP TOUGH STAINS! On TV commercials, they always threw in clothes that looked totally gross just to prove how good the detergent was. Well, here was the perfect test. I poured out the detergent, threw in the clothes, and shut the lid on the washer, pressing the ON button before leaving the room.

I went up to my room. I did not want to think about what had happened between me and Andy, so I decided to focus on my reading instead. I was frowning at the covers of books I'd chosen for their high Independent Reader points, trying to decide between *A Slow Season* and *The Long Road Ahead* when I heard a loud noise coming from the basement. *BAM-BAM-KALUNK-BAM-BAM!*

I leaped off my bed and raced toward the laundry room. The noise got louder and louder with every step. I took a deep breath and threw open the laundry room door. The washing machine rocked back and forth like it had come to life, and purple suds bubbled and frothed out from the top. I wanted to turn and race back upstairs, slamming the door behind me. But the washing machine looked like it might take off across the floor after me or explode. Or maybe both.

If I left it locked up in the basement and waited until my mom came home, there's no telling what might happen. One thing I knew for sure: Mom wasn't going to be happy about it.

So there was only one thing I could do. I closed my eyes tight and counted slowly to three. Then I flipped back the machine's lid.

Soapy foam blasted out and covered me in wet suds. It was like being sprayed by a soda bottle someone shook up and down. I scraped off the suds as the loud vibrations came to a stop and the machine grew quiet. Only then did I reach inside the bubble-filled machine.

All of a sudden my dad's voice popped into my head: *"When all else fails, read the directions."*

It was one of those sayings that usually made me roll my eyes. Dad always took such a long time reading through the directions to any new machine or gadget he bought, even when anyone could figure it out on their own. But now . . . I looked into the machine, which had turned into an overflowing bubble bath. How much soap had I put in there anyway?

I just hoped I hadn't broken the thing. If I had, I'd be in super big trouble. I tried not to think about it as I reached in and pulled out my shoes.

I gasped. My shoes were no longer pink and blue. They were pink and blue and covered in purple splotches. I had to do something, quick. I ran upstairs and dropped them in the sink. First I tried cold water. Still splotchy. Then I tried hot water. Still splotchy. Then I soaked them in warm water with some dish soap. I pulled them out ten minutes later. Still splotchy.

I stared at my shoes in shock. This purple wasn't going anywhere. Wearing mismatched shoes was cool. Wearing mismatched shoes that looked like I had spilled paint on them was definitely not.

I was in my room, looking for the other pair of mismatched shoes when the phone rang. It was Mom.

"I'm sorry, Pansy, but the meeting's running a little late. Is everything okay?"

"Fine," I lied.

"How was school?"

"Great," I lied again.

"All right, honey, I'll see you in about fifteen minutes, okay?"

As soon as I hung up the phone, I raced back to the laundry room with a handful of towels. There was soap everywhere. Well, there was nothing else for me to do but clean up the mess. After a while, I peered into the washing machine. It was still full of suds and water. I looked in a little closer and pulled out Mom's new white shirt, which was now covered in purple streaks.

Mom was going to kill me.

The only good thing about my washing experiment was that my lucky shoes were now poop-free. But they were totally ruined, and as I searched my room, I couldn't find the other pink one. I'd been so busy skating and reading and doing research that my room was a total wreck, and my extra pink shoe had disappeared underneath the mess.

As I scooped the suds into a bucket, trying to figure out how to fix the washing machine mess, the events of my day flashed into my head. I heard Andy's angry words and saw the look of hurt on his face. In my mind, I watched as he pushed back his chair and stormed out of the cafeteria, the doors swinging shut behind him.

Suddenly, the messed-up washing machine, Mom's purple-streaked shirt, and my purple-splotched mismatched shoes didn't seem like such a big deal after all.

## CHAPTER TWENTY

# Three Days

I got a big lecture when Mom came home. Just like I expected. The good news was I hadn't broken the washing machine. After Mom inspected it carefully, she said, "You put in too much soap, you mixed darks and lights, and you used hot water instead of cold. And what were you thinking adding bleach?"

I shrugged. "I thought it would make everything extra clean."

Mom shook her head, then reset the wash cycle to get rid of the water. "You know what I think, Pansy? I think it's time for you to have more responsibility around here."

"Responsibility?" I didn't like the sounds of that.

"You're almost eleven. I should have already taught you to use the washing machine."

"No, that's okay. I don't mind—"

"From now on, you'll do your own laundry once a week," Mom declared. So much for responsibility. It definitely sounded like a punishment to me.

After Mom explained how to do the laundry in great detail, I headed up to my room. I tried starting both of the boring books that I'd brought home with me, gave up, and spent the rest of the evening cleaning my room. I searched and searched, but I still couldn't find the other pink shoe.

The next morning, as I packed my purple-splotched shoes in my backpack, the phone rang. Mom told me it was Mrs. Liddell calling to say she'd be driving Andy to school for the rest of the week.

"Why?" I asked after she hung up the phone. Had Andy told his mom to call because he didn't want to walk with me anymore? "Will she be picking him up in the afternoon, too?"

"I don't know. Things are hectic at the Liddells' house right now with Anna's surgery in a few days."

"I *know* Anna's surgery's on Friday," I said. "I just don't get what that has to do with walking to school."

"I'm not sure, either," Mom said. "But I guess things could come up over the next few days, and it's probably easier to drive Andy."

"It still doesn't make sense to me," I mumbled.

My mother gave me a hug. "There are a lot of things in life that don't make sense, Pansy," she said.

As I walked to school by myself, I tried not to think about what Mom said. It was much easier to think about those shoes in my backpack, so that's what I did. Since I didn't have a matching pair of sneakers, I'd left the house in my hiking boots that morning. Luckily, Mom was too busy to ask any questions. As I changed into my purple-splotched mismatched shoes, I decided that the only way to pull the whole thing off was to act like it wasn't an accident, the way I had on the first day of school.

I walked into the classroom with a smile on my face and my head held high. Other kids smiled back at me. Miss Quetzel said, "Good morning, Pansy."

I said, "Good morning," and hung up my backpack.

Then I noticed the crowd gathered at the bulletin board. I held my breath as I walked up to the Independent Reader list. Before I could take a look, a rude voice behind me said, "Knew you couldn't hold on to first place for long." Zach bumped me with his shoulder. "What happened to you? Did someone puke grape juice all over your feet?"

That got a few laughs from Zach's buddies. I opened my mouth to say something, but nothing came out. Really, what could I tell him? That I'd stepped in dog poop and tried to wash my shoes by myself?

While I was thinking up a good answer, Zach leaned in close to me and said, "You are so weird, Pansy. Just like that Anna, the retard."

I gritted my teeth. "Anna is *not* a retard," I said. I glared at him as I clenched my fists.

But Zach just sneered at me, then laughed. "Yeah, right," he said, turning away from me as he walked to his seat.

I shot daggers with my eyes at his back. He made me so mad! I didn't even care anymore if he made fun of me. But what gave him the right to talk about Anna that way?

"Hey Pansy," Hannah called to me. "Come look."

I unclenched my fists and walked up to the list.

"Daniel took a BIG test today," Hannah said.

I stepped up to take a closer look. I'd fallen to second place, *ten* points behind Daniel.

"At least you're in second," Hannah said.

I looked at Hannah to see if she was being sarcastic. But she smiled. "That's a lot better than me," she said.

"Thanks," I said. I had no idea why Hannah was actually being nice for once. Not that it mattered. How would I ever catch up with Daniel now?

I slipped into my seat, ignoring another crack from Zach and the laughter of kids around him. I looked over at Andy, who was already seated. "Hi," I said. Andy looked up quickly and waved, then turned back to his morning work without even a hint of a smile.

The day went downhill from there. The bell rang, and Miss Quetzel announced it was time for speed drills. We only took them once a week now since a lot of people had passed all of them. I turned over my quiz and tried to focus. But the seven times tables blurred on the paper and in my mind. How could I get Andy to forgive me when he'd barely look in my direction?

*DING.* "Time's up!" Miss Quetzel said in her usual cheerful voice. I glanced down at my half-finished paper. I would never survive speed drills. On the last day of fifth grade, there would be one person still taking speed drills. Me. And I'd probably still be on the sevens.

Next, Miss Quetzel passed back our social studies tests. I chewed on the inside of my cheek before I turned it over. I hadn't studied like I should have because I was too busy reading. I definitely had to guess on some of the questions. I glanced over at Andy. He turned his paper over and shoved it in his binder so quickly I knew the grade couldn't be high. I flipped over my test to see an F staring straight at me.

Madison nudged me from behind. "I got a 98! I can't believe it! I was sure I did a terrible job! What'd you get, Pansy?"

I shook my head, folded my paper, and shoved it in my desk.

At recess, I spotted a few more pairs of mismatched shoes. Including Hannah's. I hadn't noticed her feet when we were standing by the Independent Reader scores earlier.

She was wearing one brown cowboy boot and one black one. She turned on her toes for everyone to admire her.

"Hey, what happened to your shoes?" Emma asked me after Hannah stopped spinning.

"Oh, nothing really," I said, trying to get everyone to stop looking at my feet.

Madison giggled. "Well, something happened to them, Pansy. Yesterday you didn't have purple splotches all over your feet."

"I threw them in the laundry," I said as we walked toward the playground. They were not going to leave me alone until they got an answer. "With my purple T-shirt."

Now the other girls were giggling, too.

"Why didn't you wear the *other* pink and blue pair?" Hannah asked.

"I happen to like purple," I said, and everyone laughed.

I didn't join in. It was the worst day ever. I walked right past them, even though Madison called after me, saying she liked my shoes. I ignored her, heading to the tree at the top of the hill. I dropped to the ground and leaned against the tree trunk where I sat all by myself until recess was over.

\*\*\*

When I got home that afternoon, I ran up to my room and immediately pulled on my Rollerblades. Just because I had a bad day did not mean it was time to give up on everything

I had been working toward. If I wanted to beat Zach in the skating race, I needed to get in some extra practice.

I started down the sidewalk, pushing off with one foot the way Trina had showed us on our ice skates. One foot, then the other. Arms out. Head up. And I couldn't believe it, but I started to glide. I picked up speed and made it around the block twice without falling!

"Mom! Mom, guess what!" I yelled as I pushed open the front door to the house. "I learned how to glide!"

As soon as I said the words, my Rollerblade caught on the step. My foot turned, and I pitched forward into the entryway.

Mom rushed in from the kitchen to find me sprawled across the floor. "What in the world?" She reached out a hand to help me up. "Why are you wearing your skates in the house?"

I rolled over and dragged my feet inside. "I guess I forgot. I learned to glide on one foot! You have to learn to glide if you want to go fast—"

"So you decided to wait until you were inside to fall?" Mom joked.

I didn't feel like laughing, though. I sucked in my breath as I unlaced the boot that had gotten caught on the top step. "Ouch."

"Here, let me take a look." Mom kneeled down next to me and pulled the boot off. I groaned. She took off my sock. I howled. Mom frowned. "Hmm . . . looks like you might have sprained your ankle."

"Sprained my ankle? How? OUCH!" I howled again when Mom touched my ankle.

"You must have turned it when you fell. Let me get some ice."

"My ankle's not sprained!" I called after her. But it sure did hurt. Mom helped me over to a chair and stuck my foot in a bowl of ice. Half an hour later, my ankle had swollen to the size of a tangerine. I couldn't really tell if I had an ankle bone anymore.

I pulled my foot out of the icy bowl and hobbled around the room.

"I'm taking you to the doctor, just to be sure you didn't break it," Mom said.

"I'm fine!" I protested.

Mom ignored me, picking up her car keys and purse.

After sitting in the waiting room for over an hour, the doctor said I had a twisted ankle and told me to stay off it for a few days or longer depending on how fast it was healing.

"You never can tell with these things," the doctor said.

"What do you mean?" I asked him. I couldn't miss my skating lesson that weekend. We were going to work on one-foot glides and practice racing. "I'll be better by Saturday, won't I?"

The doctor shook his head. "I doubt you'll be completely healed by Saturday. You can rent crutches in rehab downstairs," he told my mom. "Just make sure she stays off that foot."

"Crutches?" This was starting to sound serious. "But I thought you said it was just a twisted ankle!"

"It is," the doctor said. "You won't need a cast. But you'll need to keep the weight off your ankle. It could take a couple of weeks, maybe longer, to be completely healed."

"A COUPLE OF WEEKS!" I'd worked so hard, survived endless crashes and skinned knees—had it all been a complete waste of time? Instead of skating with Anna at the Good Citizens party, I'd be standing on the sidelines, leaning on a pair of crutches.

"Come on, honey," Mom said. "You'll have fun swinging around on crutches."

I was *not* going to have fun swinging around on crutches. Zach would have another excuse to make fun of me, I was missing the most important weeks of skating practice, and I might even have to sit out at the Good Citizens party.

I thought about how I'd fallen to second place in Independent Reader, how I'd flunked a social studies quiz, how I couldn't get past the sevens in speed drills, and how Andy was barely speaking to me. It was like I was letting Anna down all over again, the same way I had when I chickened out of Locks of Love and backed out of Girl Scout camp. I stared down at my swollen ankle, and all I could see was my quest for extraordinary crumbling before my eyes.

CHAPTER TWENTY-ONE

# One Day

I spent the rest of the afternoon in my room. I didn't open a book to read, I didn't study for my social studies test, and I sure didn't go outside and practice roller-blading. Instead, I flopped down on my bed the best I could with a hurt ankle and tried to wipe my mind clean, like a brand new whiteboard.

I'd watched Mom do her yoga and meditation DVDs enough times to know that the first thing I had to do was breathe in and out. Slowly.

"Concentrate on your breath," the man with the soothing voice on the screen always said.

So I did, and surprise, surprise, I fell fast asleep. A twisted ankle can zap the energy right out of you.

When I woke up the next morning, I suddenly felt a lot better. I never believed it when Mom said, "Things will look brighter in the morning," but this time she was right. I glanced over at my calendar, where I'd circled December 2 with a sparkly glittery pen. Anna's surgery was only a day away, and I wasn't about to let a little setback like a twisted ankle get in the way of becoming extraordinary.

Mom, of course, had to drive me to school. When I showed up with crutches, everyone gathered around, waiting to hear what happened. So I tried to make it exciting. "I guess I got a little too much speed on my skates," I told the other kids. "I was going super-fast." Then I let Madison and some of the other girls try out my crutches. Zach made a few jokes, which I totally ignored.

That afternoon, I went straight up to my room, hoping to get a little ahead on my reading since skating practice wasn't taking up my time for now. When I made my way downstairs later that afternoon, a delicious smell greeted me. I took a good whiff and knew right away what was cooking—Mom's special lasagna.

I peeked in the oven at the cheese bubbling over the casserole dish. "Mmmm, yum. When are we eating?"

"Sorry, hon," Mom said. "The lasagna's for the Liddells. They'll be busy over the next few weeks so I made something they could keep in the freezer and heat up when needed." Mom took out the casserole dish and turned off the oven.

I leaned my crutches against the table and dropped into a chair.

"We'll bring it over tonight so we can visit with Anna before her surgery," Mom said.

"Andy will like the lasagna. It's his favorite food."

"That's what I figured," Mom said as she scrubbed a pot in the sink. "I'm sure Andy will be glad to see you, too."

"I don't know about that," I said.

"What are you talking about?" Mom dropped the sponge into the sink and turned to face me.

I shrugged, not wanting to tell her about the fight we had or about the way Andy had been working on Zeraclop City with Daniel. "He's hardly talked to me this week, that's all."

"Poor Andy," Mom said, shaking her head. "I'm sure he's worried about Anna's surgery this Friday. He just has to deal with things his own way. I hope you'll be very understanding over the next couple of weeks. That's what he needs more than anything right now."

"I'm trying to, Mom. But he hasn't been very nice to me lately."

"Honey, I'm sure this has nothing to do with you. Maybe he's trying to tell you that he has a lot on his mind."

I thought about it for a minute. "Because of the surgery? I thought he'd be happy about it, that Anna'll stop having seizures all the time. She won't even have to wear the helmet anymore."

"Pansy . . ." Mom dried her hands on a towel and sat down next to me. "The Liddells have had a very difficult decision to make. They want to stop Anna's seizures, yet they know this surgery is a huge risk. Do you understand what I mean by a huge risk?"

I shook my head. "You mean it might not work? Could it make the seizures worse?"

"It's more than that." Mom paused and drew her lips together like she was trying to make a decision. "Your father and I wondered if we should tell you. But you're almost eleven, old enough to hear the truth. I'm sure Andy knows, which may explain the way he's been acting lately." Mom placed a hand under my chin. She turned my head so that I was looking into her eyes. "Anna could die," she said softly.

"Wh-what?"

"Brain surgery carries a huge risk. Some people don't make it through the procedure. Some make it but then die of infection weeks later."

"No!" I pulled myself to my feet and shook my head. Large black letters etched across my mind. *Anna could die.* The room was closing in on me. "Anna is not going to die. The surgery's going to make her better!"

"We're all hoping for the best. The Liddells have talked to the best specialists, and they have high hopes. Anna is a strong girl, a fighter, and they really believe this surgery can stop or at least minimize the seizures."

I stood there, not knowing what to think. I swallowed back sobs. Feeling shaky and unsteady on my feet, I picked up my crutches and turned to go back up the stairs.

"The Liddells need us right now," Mom called after me. "Be a good friend to Andy. He needs you now, more than ever."

I swiped at a tear and continued up the steps. *Anna is strong!* I wanted to shout at my mother. *She'll make it through this surgery, and she'll be herself again. Just you wait and see!*

*** 

Later that evening, we stood outside the Liddells' house with the still-warm lasagna. Andy opened the door and reached for the foil-wrapped dish as if he was expecting it.

"Thanks, Mrs. Smith," he said, placing the dish on the counter without even a glance in my direction. "Mom's in Anna's room. She just finished shaving Anna's head. She's bald as a bowling ball!"

Was he trying to make a joke? Andy's words echoed in the room.

I followed him down the familiar hall. I stopped in Anna's doorway, unable to go inside. Andy hadn't been joking. Anna was bald! Without her beautiful copper hair, Anna looked pale and skinny as she lay against her pillows. She looked just like one of those cancer patients on TV.

"Hi, Anna." My voice came out in a whisper.

"I think she lost ten pounds, all in hair," Mrs. Liddell said. I guess she was trying to make a joke, too. Maybe they were all trying hard to act like what was going on wasn't big-time serious. But it wasn't working.

I couldn't even make my lips curve up in a little smile. I pulled a small box out of my jacket pocket. "I brought you a present, Anna," I said, trying to keep my voice steady. I looked over at Andy. His eyes dropped to the box in my hands. I looked up at Mrs. Liddell. "Do you want me to open it for her?"

"Please."

Everyone stood silently as I tore off the wrapping paper. Right before we left the house, I thought of something I wanted to give Anna before she went into surgery. I took off the lid and pulled out the cooking badge I'd earned by baking those oatmeal chocolate chip cookies.

After Anna got better, she could earn her own badges. But, for now, I wanted her to have it, to let her know I'd changed.

"It's for your vest," I said to Anna.

I heard someone suck in a breath. Was it Mrs. Liddell? Or had it been Andy?

"That's so sweet of you, Pansy," Mrs. Liddell said as Anna took the badge from me and closed her fingers around it tightly. Mom reached over and squeezed my hand.

Anna looked up at me and smiled. Her eyes sparkled. She made a long sound, and I laughed. Everyone probably thought it was strange that I was laughing when Anna was lying in front of me with her head shaved, getting ready to go to the hospital for a surgery where they cut her brain open.

But when Anna smiled, it really made me happy inside. Anna knew what I had done for her. I was sure of it.

Still looking into my eyes, Anna made another long cheerful sound.

"She's saying 'thank you,'" Mrs. Liddell said, her eyes shining. "You're a good friend, Pansy."

"Thanks," I said. "Anna deserves it. She's the best friend anyone could have."

\*\*\*

"I don't want to go to school tomorrow," I told my parents when we got home from the Liddells'. I'd finally figured out a way to make things right between Andy and me again. "I want to spend the day at the hospital, with Andy."

My parents exchanged looks. Then Mom said, "I know Andy would love to have some company, but—"

"I need to be there for Anna, too."

"Anna already knows how much you care about her," Mom said. "And she'll be in surgery the whole time. As soon as she can have visitors, I'll bring you to the hospital."

I shook my head. A loyal friend would be there during the whole thing. I knew she was counting on me.

"I'm not going to school tomorrow."

Silence. My parents questioned each other with their eyes.

"I'm sure it'll be an excused absence," I said.

"Your mom and I are going to work tomorrow." My dad took off his glasses and lay them on the table next to him, then rubbed his eyes. "We can't stay with you at the hospital, and Anna's parents will have enough to worry about without having to watch an extra child."

I groaned. "Dad, they're not going to have to watch me. I'm not a baby, you know." It would be perfect. Andy would take one look at me, and we'd both forget all about our stupid fight. I'd bring tons of stuff to keep us busy— comic books and my Games on the Go set.

My mom was shaking her head. "Pansy, I know how much you want to be there for your friends, but I'm not going to let you spend the day at the hospital."

I protested. I begged. I whined. Finally, I started to cry. How was I going to get through a whole day of school while Anna was at the hospital, lying on an operating table as they cut open her brain?

Mom put her arm around me and told me everything was going to be okay. But that's not what she had said a few hours ago. Suddenly, I felt exhausted, like every bit of energy had drained right out of me. I wiped my eyes and forced my feet to move up the steps. When I got to my room, I collapsed onto the bed, falling asleep without even changing into my pajamas.

## CHAPTER TWENTY-TWO

# Zero Days, December 2

Friday, December 2, dragged on and on. I tried to act like it was a normal day. I smiled at my friends and let my classmates swing around on my crutches. I sat up tall in my seat and tried my best to pay attention during class. But whenever I glanced over at Andy's empty desk next to me, my mind wandered. What was Andy doing all day at the hospital? Was he sad that I wasn't there with him?

I pictured Mr. and Mrs. Liddell sipping from those Styrofoam cups of coffee. Maybe they'd let Andy have a soda as a special treat, even though it was only ten in the morning and they never had soda at their house. I could imagine neighbors and friends stopping by to sit with them. Even Mom had said she would stop by at lunchtime and see how things were going.

Andy probably had a pile of books with him. Definitely his Zeraclop notebook. Maybe his parents would let him explore the hospital, ride up and down in the elevators, and visit the gift shop.

As long as my school day was feeling, I knew Andy's wait in the hospital must be feeling even longer.

***

"Where's Andy today?" Emma asked at lunchtime. "Don't you usually walk to school together?"

"Usually," I said. "But we haven't walked together this week."

"Walking to school on crutches would take a really long time, I bet," Hannah said. "How long do you have to stay on them, anyway?"

"Until my ankle heals," I said, happy that I didn't have to explain the real reason Andy and I hadn't been walking together. "The doctor said it could take a few days . . . or even a few weeks."

Madison's eyes widened. "A few weeks? Oh, Pansy, you just have to get better by the skating party!"

"I will," I said, pretending like I believed what I said.

The afternoon crawled by even slower than the morning. I kept staring at the hands of the clock, trying to make them move forward with my mind. Finally, the last bell rang, and we lined up for dismissal.

I leaned on my crutches as I waited for Mom to pick me up. It was three thirty. Anna's surgery should've been over by then—unless something had gone wrong.

I clenched my teeth and felt the muscles all over my body tense up. *Hurry up, Mom . . . can't you be on time on a day like this?*

I almost dropped my crutches and ran for the car when I spotted Mom's dark blue Honda.

"How is Anna?" I asked as soon as I opened the door. "Is the operation over? Is she okay? When can I see her?"

"Hold on a minute," Mom said with a laugh, and that's when the knot in my stomach began to unwind. I placed my crutches on the floor in the backseat and climbed in. Mom smiled back at me. "Anna's doing great! Get buckled in and I'll tell you all about it."

My muscles loosened, and I exhaled a gush of air, as though I'd been holding my breath all day. "When did the surgery finish? What did the doctor say? Have you seen her yet?"

"It was a long surgery and only finished an hour ago. I stopped by the hospital at lunchtime—"

"How's Andy doing? Did you talk to him?"

"Andy's okay. I'm sure he would have loved to have your company—"

"You should have let me go, Mom! It's not like I learned anything today. All I could think about was Anna."

"I know, honey." Mom glanced up at me in the rearview mirror. "But your dad and I had to make a decision, and we thought it was best for you to go to school. Anyway, the good news is that the surgery went well. Anna should be in the recovery room for the next few hours."

"So, we can visit her today?"

Mom shook her head. "Definitely not today. Andy hasn't even been in to see her yet. She's under heavy anesthesia. It'll be a while before she wakes up."

"Tomorrow, then."

"She'll be in intensive care for a while—"

"Anna is strong," I said. "I bet she'll be out of intensive care and out of the hospital sooner than anyone thinks."

"Pansy, it's going to take time," Mom said, launching into a detailed medical explanation of Anna's recovery. But I wasn't listening. I knew it! I believed in Anna, just like she believed in me, and she made it through the surgery without a problem! Over the next few days, Anna would start to heal. I was sure of it, just like I knew that when Anna found out how I'd changed, she'd forgive me. And this time she'd be the one to put on her own necklace, and she'd know exactly what it meant.

## CHAPTER TWENTY-THREE

# December 7

I didn't get to visit Anna over the weekend. Mom said we had to wait until Anna was stronger—that there was always the risk of infection after major surgery, that Anna was in good hands, and that we had to be patient.

Finally, on Wednesday after school, I heard the words I'd been waiting for.

"Mrs. Liddell says Anna's vital signs have stabilized," Mom told me when I got home that afternoon. "Would you like to visit her this evening?"

"You bet!" I shouted. "Hooray!"

I got to work right away making a card for Anna. I wrote GET WELL, ANNA! in silver glitter glue on the front. Inside, I pasted pictures of Anna's favorite things: a swimming pool, a rainbow, tennis shoes, someone pumping her legs on a swing set, a basket full of puppies, a plateful of cookies . . .

Wait a second. Why hadn't I thought of it before?

"I've got the perfect present for Anna," I said to Mom. "Oreos."

"Hmm." Mom looked up from her laptop and frowned. "Anna doesn't have much of an appetite, according to Mrs. Liddell. She still has a feeding tube in to make sure she gets enough nutrients."

"But she's eating hospital food, too, right?"

"They're working very hard to get her to eat three meals a day. Most of what she's eating is soft, like yogurt and cottage cheese."

"She'll eat the cookies," I said. Anna used to eat them every day after lunch. "Oreos are her favorite cookie."

"Even so, how about some balloons, instead?"

"We can bring balloons along with the Oreos."

Mom smiled. "Whatever you want."

After dinner, we stopped at the store for the cookies and a big pink balloon that read GET WELL SOON! I bubbled over with excitement the whole ride to the hospital.

But when we entered the hospital lobby, the knot in my stomach returned. As we stepped into the elevator, I looked away from the wrinkled woman in a wheelchair, a bag of IV fluids hooked to her arm with needles.

I tried to ignore the nurses who rushed past us in the hallway with scary-looking carts, and I plugged my ears to drown out the weeping coming from inside one of the rooms we passed. I breathed through my mouth so I wouldn't have to take in the horrible smell of chemicals mixed with sickness.

I hobbled past my parents, crutch-free, and knocked on the door to Room 1103—Anna's room.

Mrs. Liddell opened the door and smiled when she saw me.

"Hi, Pansy!" She poked her head out and waved at my parents. "I was just feeding Anna dinner. Come on in."

Andy sat in a chair next to the bed. He flicked off the TV with a remote, looked at me, and waved. But he didn't wave the way you would at a really good friend who you were glad to see. It was more like a greeting for a stranger, someone you barely knew.

I waved back, then turned my attention to Anna, who was lying on the bed.

I knew something was wrong right away. Anna was so still and quiet that I would have thought she was asleep. But she was awake, staring at the TV, which wasn't even on.

"Hi, Anna." I tried to make my voice sound cheerful, but it came out forced and strained. Not my voice at all. I tried a smile, but my lips only trembled as I leaned over to give her a hug.

Anna didn't hug back. She didn't make a happy sound like she usually did when she saw me. She didn't smile. She didn't even look into my eyes.

She just lay there, her head drooping down, her eyes looking lifeless. She didn't seem to care if I was there or not.

I swallowed. I tried to keep my voice steady as I tied the balloon to the end of the bed. "I brought you a balloon, Anna," I said. Then I placed the box of Oreos on top of her blanket. "And cookies." I tore open the wrapper. "Look, Anna. Oreos—they're your favorite!"

Then Anna turned her head. Her eyes flickered as she stared at the package of cookies. She lifted her hand and dropped it on top of the package. There was silence, except for the sound of crackling plastic as Anna's hand landed on the package.

The sound filled the room and roared in my ears. I blinked a few times to make sure I was seeing things clearly. Anna was supposed to eat those cookies, not hit them!

"I can't believe it!" Mrs. Liddell said. "Look, Andy! She's using her right hand!"

Andy jumped up from his chair. "Do it again, Anna," he said. "You can do it."

When Anna hit the package again, Mrs. Liddell clapped and cheered. "We were worried that the surgery had affected the right side of her body," she explained. "This is the first time she's moved her right hand since last Friday!"

"It was Pansy's idea to bring the Oreos," Dad said. "Seems like it was a good one."

I heard my name, but I couldn't speak. The conversation in the background melted into sounds in slow-motion, muffled background noise. People were talking and laughing and smiling, but I couldn't understand what they were saying.

All I saw was Anna. Lifting her arm with determination, dropping it back down on the package of cookies. In a flash, I rewound to last April, the first time I'd seen Anna since she left for camp. Mom had warned me that the brain damage had changed her, but I didn't believe her until I saw her lying in that hospital bed.

"Hi, Anna," I had said, handing her the stuffed puppy I'd picked out for her. It had light blonde fur and big brown eyes, like her golden retriever who had died a few months before, and it had a blue ribbon around its neck, since blue was her favorite color.

Anna had looked up at me, but her expression didn't change. Like she had no idea who I was. Her eyes, which used to sparkle with energy, had stared back at me blankly.

"It's Pansy," I had said in a voice that shook. "Remember me?"

"Of course she remembers you," Mrs. Liddell had said softly. "She'll always remember her best friend."

The room shifted back into focus.

"This is just wonderful!" Mrs. Liddell said. "If Anna's moving her hand, then she may move her leg again soon!"

My legs felt like strands of spaghetti. I put my hand on a chair to hold myself steady.

I stared at Anna, who was still concentrating on the Oreos. She was pale—paler than she'd been when I visited her before the surgery. She was hooked up to monitors and IVs, and her shaved head was wrapped in bandages.

I glanced over at Andy. He was staring at Anna, too. For a moment, he looked over at me, and our eyes met before he quickly looked away. But I'd seen it—the emptiness in his eyes that hadn't been there before.

It took all of my concentration to stand perfectly still and breathe. Breathe in, breathe out. Breathe in, breathe out. I'd imagined it all—Anna understanding my words when I told her about my goals, Anna looking at my badge and getting that I'd earned it for her. Now I knew that Anna hadn't understood that I was doing any of those things for her.

All my dreams about Anna's recovery instantly evaporated into the air. They were just dreams. That's all they ever were.

The girl lying on the bed next to me was just the outside shell of what she used to be, kind of like those empty shells you find on the beach after the creature on the inside has already moved on.

I wanted to run out of Anna's room, down the eleven flights of steps, and out the front doors. Just run, run, run, far enough away that I could stop seeing my best friend lying in a hospital bed—my best friend Anna, who could look right at me and not see me at all.

## CHAPTER TWENTY-FOUR

# December 7

I was quiet all the way home from the hospital. Mom and Dad filled the silence. They babbled away about how great Anna was doing, how the surgery was going to help with her seizures, how her body was strong, and how she'd be walking again before we knew it.

I just sat in the backseat with an ache in my chest that hurt every time I inhaled.

When we got home, I went straight up to my room and shut the door. First thing I did was open my closet and pull my mismatched purple-splotched shoes from their hiding place. I tossed them as hard as I could against the wall, and they bounced off and clunked to the floor. Next, I picked up the Independent Reader book on my desk and hurled it across the room. It flipped over once and landed facedown with the pages open. I picked up the other book from my desk, a hardcover I'd chosen because of the points it would give me. I threw it, the book hitting my dresser and landing with a thud.

There was a knock on my door. "Pansy? Are you all right?"

"I'm fine, Mom!" I called back through the closed door.

My Girl Scout vest hung on the back of my chair. I picked that up and threw it, too. Finally, I spotted my Rollerblades in a corner by my desk. With all my strength, I hurled them as far as I could. One hit the wall, denting it; the other hit the bed. *Ka-thunk.*

There was a knock on the door again. "Pansy! What is going on in there?"

"Nothing, Mom," I said, but my voice came out all garbled and wobbly.

"Open the door, Pansy. I need to talk to you."

So I opened the door. Mom's eyebrows curved down in a worried expression. "Are you okay?" she asked in a quiet voice.

"I'm fine." I dropped down on my bed, trying to cover up a sniffle with a fake cough.

Mom sat next to me. "Well, you don't seem fine to me."

I kicked my foot against the bed. Which hurt, since my foot was still sore. So I kicked the bed again, this time with the other foot.

Mom lowered her voice. She ran her hand across my hair. "Honey, I know it was hard seeing Anna in the hospital tonight."

I stared down at my rainbow-colored rug.

"Anna's been through a lot, and she's proven how strong she is," Mom continued. "She just needs some time to recover."

"Recover? She's never going to be *Anna* again!" I burst out.

Mom paused. "Oh, sweetheart. I know how tough all of this has been for you."

I didn't say anything. Mom sighed, like she didn't know the right thing to say either. But when she didn't move from her spot, I knew we were playing a waiting game, and I was going to lose. Mom would sit there all night until I started talking.

"I'm giving up," I finally said, meeting her gaze. "I was trying to be an extraordinary person for Anna, but I failed. Not that it matters to her anyway. So I'm done. From now on, I'm just going to be ordinary old Pansy again."

Mom gave me a hard look, then said, "I'd certainly never call you ordinary. Is that what all this was about? The roller-blading? Joining Girl Scouts? The reading contest? You were trying to be extraordinary for Anna's sake?"

I nodded. I'd worked so hard—for *nothing*. I finally saw the complete and total truth: Anna would never recover. She'd never know that I'd done anything for her—that I was trying to make up for all the stupid ways I'd let her down before.

"There's nothing wrong with trying to improve yourself," Mom said. "I'm proud of you for trying to make straight A's and for trying to win the reading contest."

"I could read day and night, and Daniel Walker would still earn more points than me."

"You shouldn't worry about Daniel Walker. You should be proud of your own accomplishments, of all the points *you've* earned."

"Who cares if I earn a bunch of points if I'm not the best at it?"

"No one said you have to be the best. It's hard being number one at anything."

I rolled my eyes. The only reason I'd even come close to first place was because of that summer reading book I'd taken a test on, and all the easy books I had read in addition to the novels. That made me a cheater, didn't it? I didn't even bother to bring that up.

"What about your ice-skating lessons? You've been doing so well. Your ankle will heal, and you'll pick right up where you left off."

"I was only doing it because of the Good Citizens party in a couple of weeks," I said. *Which I'm not going to. Why would I go to a stupid ice-skating party if Anna isn't going to be there with me?*

"But you made great progress. You worked so hard!" Mom picked up my Girl Scout vest. "I hope you're not quitting Girl Scouts, too."

"Who cares about Girl Scouts?" I said. I'd given my badge to Anna, and she had no idea what it was! "I'm not going on any scary camping trips. I'm not any braver than I used to be."

"But you're trying." Mom stood up and hung the vest over the back of my desk chair. "That's the main thing. You're out there, and you're making new friends—"

"I don't need any new friends."

My mom sat back on the bed next to me. For a moment she didn't say anything. When she spoke, her voice was quieter than it had been before. "You know what, Pansy? You do need new friends. It's okay to have more than one best friend, you know."

I picked up my teddy bear and held it close. I wasn't ready to think about new friends. All I wanted to do was curl up under the covers and make the pain I felt go away. Instead, I could sense the ache inside me from losing Anna growing bigger and bigger until I thought it might swallow me whole.

Mom put her arms around me and gave me a hug. "Anna would want you to have friends."

Something burst inside of me when I heard those words. I wiggled out of my mom's arms. The teddy bear fell to the floor. "I don't want new friends, Mom! I want Anna!"

"Oh, honey . . ." Mom's voice broke. "I'm so sorry. Maybe someday there will be a way for a doctor to cure someone who has severe brain damage. But for now, this is the best anyone can hope for."

"How can you say that, Mom?" My voice rang out in my ears, as if it were coming from somewhere else. "You saw Anna today. She couldn't even look me in the eyes. She couldn't smile. She can't get out of bed, and she can't walk or make sounds like she used to, and the only thing she could do was hit the Oreos with her hand. Are you saying that's all Andy and his parents were hoping for?"

"Anna moved her right hand for the first time in almost a week. I told you, it takes a while to recover from a surgery like this—"

I took a deep breath and glanced around the room. I wished I had more than a Girl Scout vest or a book or a pair of skates to throw. What I needed was a big glass vase or pitcher, something that would go *CRASH*! and splinter into a million pieces when it hit the wall. But there was nothing breakable in my room. So I kicked my unhurt foot against the bed again, as hard as I could. "So, if Anna recovers, then in a few weeks, or a few months, she'll be back to the way she was before the surgery? You think the Liddells should be happy about that?"

"The Liddells *are* happy—" Mom started to say, but I didn't give her a chance to finish.

The words burst from me like a gushing fountain, words I'd kept inside for almost eight months: "The *old* Anna used to laugh and play sports and tell funny stories, she made straight A's and helped anyone out who needed it and was nice to everyone, and now . . . she's gone. The *new* Anna—the one who made it through the surgery—can't talk to you or understand what you're saying, she can't read or write or do much of anything except spin her dumb toys around and around and make funny noises. She doesn't even know when someone is working hard to do things just for her! She used to take care of everyone else, and now she can't even take care of herself! And you're saying the Liddells are *happy* now?"

Mom nodded, then reached for my hand. "The surgery was a success. Anna hasn't had any seizures, and even more importantly"—she squeezed my hand— "Anna's alive. I told you about the risks of the surgery, and she came through just fine. The Liddells have had time to get used to the changes, and I think they've accepted the Anna she's become—"

"Well, I don't accept her!" I yanked my hand away from my mom's, reaching for my Best Friends necklace. I pulled. Hard. The chain stung my skin as it snapped apart and fell in my lap. I picked it up and threw it across the room with all my strength. It clanked against my dresser and slid to the floor.

"Pansy, I'm so sorry," my mom said again. She put her arm around me, and this time I didn't pull away.

I wished I were a little girl, back when my mother could make everything all right. I would lean my head on her shoulder, and she'd wrap her arms around me and brush my tears away. She could fix anything with a hug and her soft words—a skinned knee, a fight with a friend, a terrible day at school.

But there was nothing Mom could do to bring Anna back. There was nothing anyone could do. Anna never did anything bad to anyone, and something horrible had happened to her. That's not the way it was supposed to work! If you're a good person, good things should happen to you. I always believed that my Anna was still in there somewhere, and I just needed to find a way to reach her.

Now I knew the truth. Anna was gone, and the girl left in her place didn't understand a thing. There wasn't a magical connection between us. And there was no such thing as miracles.

Something broke inside as I felt my mom's arms embrace me. Hot, angry tears burned from my eyes, and I could hardly catch my breath. I shut my eyes and collapsed against her, my sobs filling the room.

## CHAPTER TWENTY-FIVE

# December 8

B efore we get started this morning," Miss Quetzel
announced after the bell rang, "I have some news
to share. Some of you may have noticed that Andy has
been absent for the last few days, and he's not here today,
either. That's because his twin sister, Anna, had brain
surgery last Friday."

A hush fell over the classroom. I gulped in some air and
let it out slowly, waiting for Miss Quetzel to continue.

"I spoke with Andy's mother last night, and Anna is
doing fine. I thought it would be nice for the class to make
some cards for Anna." Miss Quetzel smiled. "When Andy
returns in a few days, it will make him feel better to know
how much we all care about him, and about Anna, too."

The classroom filled with the sounds of people pulling out markers and crayons and talking about Anna and Andy. Madison tapped my shoulder. When I turned around, she whispered, "Why didn't you tell me about the surgery? Didn't Andy want anyone to know?"

I shrugged and turned back around in my seat quickly, my cheeks feeling hot. I got busy lining up markers on my desk, ignoring Madison even though she kept asking me questions. I forced myself to fill the paper with happy pictures, pretending I didn't know that Anna wouldn't understand it was a get-well card and that I had made it myself. I drew balloons and flowers with smiley faces and lots of butterflies.

Butterflies. Back in second grade, Anna had to draw a butterfly on her insect poster. She was good at almost everything, but she sure couldn't draw a butterfly.

"I'll draw one for you," I had offered.

Anna had shook her head and began to go over her outline with a black marker. "Thanks, Pansy. But I can do it myself. It doesn't have to be perfect, you know."

When she was finished, we both had sat there, studying her drawing. It was definitely not perfect—unless you called it perfectly awful. Lopsided wings stuck to a crooked body covered with funny-looking spots.

"You should have let me draw it," I had said.

"It's not that bad," Anna had said back. "It'll look a lot better once I color it."

"I'd start over, if I were you."

"Well, you're not me. And I think it looks just fine."

I'd snorted, but Anna had ignored me, coloring happily with her markers. I couldn't believe it. Wasn't she embarrassed to turn in a poster that looked like it had been drawn by a preschooler?

"I wish I were a good artist like you," Anna had said later, when Mrs. Cunningham hung her butterfly next to my caterpillar poster.

"I'm not a good artist," I had told her. "Caterpillars and butterflies are easy to draw, that's all."

"Not easy for everyone," Anna had said with a laugh. "Just look at my butterfly!"

I stared down at the butterfly I'd drawn on the get-well card, a colorful blend of blue, lavender, pink, and yellow. Anna would not look at the butterfly and remember the one she'd drawn back in second grade and the conversation we'd had. She wouldn't look at the smiley face and think about the matching T-shirts we'd bought at the beach the summer after third grade, blue with big yellow smiley faces in the middle. She wouldn't look at the flowers and think about the flower decals we'd stuck all over the walls of her room.

Anna wouldn't know or care that the card was from me, Pansy Smith, who used to be her very best friend in the world.

***

"So, what happened?" Madison asked me as we sat down for lunch. "My mom said there isn't a cure for brain damage—"

"There's not," Hannah said.

"But Anna just had brain surgery!" Madison said. "Did the doctors fix Anna's brain?"

"Yeah," Emma said. "I've been waiting all morning to find out. Is Anna going to be okay? Is she coming back to our school? I bet Andy's so excited."

"No," I finally said. I looked down at my purple-splotched shoes. "I mean, Anna's going to be okay. But there's nothing they can do about her brain damage. They were just trying to stop her seizures."

"Oh," Madison said, and silence fell across our end of the table. Even Hannah kept her mouth shut.

After a while, Madison put her hand on my shoulder. "I'm sorry, Pansy," she said quietly.

I nodded, unable to think of anything to say. Soon the girls started talking about other things, but I didn't join in the conversation. I sat there in silence, eating my lunch, even though I didn't taste a bite.

At the end of the day, I walked up to Miss Quetzel's desk to get Andy's homework as his mom had asked me to do. "Can I take the cards, too?" I asked her. "Since I'm bringing his work anyway?"

Miss Quetzel smiled. "That would be nice, Pansy," she said as she handed me a manila envelope with the cards inside.

***

I took the envelope up to my room when I got home. The cards were colorful and full of sunshine, like Miss Quetzel said they should be. I noticed there wasn't one from Zach, which suited me fine. Anna didn't need a card from him.

A little while later, I made my way downstairs. I'd been off the crutches for the last few days. Maybe it was time for a walk. It was definitely time to visit Andy. I'd give him the cards and the homework assignments, and it could be like a peace treaty between us.

"Mom? Our class made some cards for Anna today. Can I take them over to Andy's?"

My mother stepped out from the kitchen, a towel in her hand. "Honey, Andy's not home."

I stopped with my hand on the front door. "Oh. I guess they're at the hospital again." I sighed. The longer I waited, the bigger the gap seemed to grow between Andy and me. I wanted to fix things between us before it was too late. "I could leave it on the front porch. His homework, too."

Mom shook her head. "Andy's staying with his grandmother this week. I just spoke with his mom a few minutes ago."

I dropped the books and envelope on a chair. "Why? And when's he coming back to school?"

"Andy's mom said things are too hectic right now. She's been spending the night in the hospital with Anna, so she thought it would be better if he stayed with his grandma.

But they're planning on sending Anna home this weekend, so he'll be back at school on Monday."

I chewed the inside of my cheek. I wanted to feel happy that Anna was strong enough to leave the hospital. Instead, I felt that dull ache inside of me again, that ache that just wouldn't go away.

"Your foot must feel better if you were planning to walk to Andy's."

I nodded. "I think it's mostly healed."

"Let's go for a walk, then," Mom suggested. "It's a beautiful day, and it'll be good to get some exercise. Let me just change—"

"No, that's all right," I said as I headed toward the door. "I think I'll go for a walk by myself."

"Are you sure? It will just take me a minute to get my tennis shoes on."

"That's okay, Mom," I said, even though I could see in her eyes how much she wanted to go with me. "I'd rather go by myself."

CHAPTER TWENTY-SIX

# December 9

A new set of Independent Reader scores was posted in the morning. I was now twenty points behind Daniel, who'd finished another thick fantasy book the night before. I hadn't taken a single test since Anna's surgery.

"Did you see the list?" Hannah asked me as we lined up to go to the library. "Don't feel bad, Pansy. You're doing great. It's impossible keeping up with Daniel—he's a genius."

"I'm not trying to keep up with anyone," I told her.

"That's because you never could," Zach Turansky butted in. "Daniel was cutting you some slack for a while. Watch him take off now. He'll leave you in the dust! *Buuuurrrrrrrr!*"

"It doesn't matter. I don't care if I'm not in first place," I said. Anna didn't care, so why should I? Zach was too busy *buuuurrrring* to listen. Some of the other kids laughed. Facing Zach was the last thing I felt like doing. I looked around for Miss Quetzel, but she'd stepped out to the hall to talk to the other fifth-grade teacher.

"Hey, Pansy, maybe you should get some *brain* surgery," Zach said. "You could get a brain transplant. That's the only way you'd be smart enough to beat Daniel Walker."

I spun around and stared straight at him. "Brain surgery? Are you joking about *brain surgery?*"

"Yeah," he continued in his smart-alecky tone. "I was thinking an operation might help you."

I narrowed my eyes. "Do you know what it's like when your best friend becomes brain-damaged? Or your twin?"

Zach held his hands out in front of him. "Whoa . . . I didn't say anything about brain damage. I didn't say anything about Anna—"

"Not this time. But you have before." I lowered my voice. "Anna is *not* retarded. She got sick, and the sickness damaged her brain. It could have happened to anyone. It could have happened to *you*—"

"Okay, okay, I get it," Zach said, backing away from me.

"No, you don't get it at all!" I said, and this time no one interrupted me. Not even Zach. "There's no cure for brain damage. It's like starting over, except you're stuck in this place where you can't get any better. It doesn't matter how smart you used to be, how good you were at everything, there's nothing anyone can do. And then you get seizures, so they have to do brain surgery. Do you know what happens during brain surgery? First, they shave off all your hair. Then they cut open your head and operate on you for hours. You lose a lot of blood. You can get infections. Your family sits in the waiting room and prays for you." I stopped and took a deep breath.

A group of kids had gathered around us, silent, listening.

"You can die from brain surgery," I whispered. "I wouldn't wish it on anyone. Not even you, Zach Turansky."

For the first time ever, Zach looked like he didn't know what to say. He opened his mouth, shut it, then opened it again. When he spoke, some of the meanness in his voice had disappeared. Not a lot. Some people might not even notice. But I did.

"I was just kidding," Zach finally said. "No big deal, okay?"

My fists shook.

"Who cares what Zach thinks?" Madison whispered in my ear. She put her arm around my shoulder and led me to the back of the line. "It doesn't matter about Independent Reader anyway. I'm in tenth place!"

I'd completely forgotten that the whole thing started because of Independent Reader. My heart was pounding.

I'd stood up to Zach Turansky. I'd stood up for Anna and said what I should have said months ago.

Daniel slipped in line behind me. I felt a light punch on my shoulder. "Way to go," he said quietly.

I took another deep breath and pulled back my shoulders.

Anna would be proud of me for trying so hard in the reading contest. But she'd be even more proud if she could have heard what I finally said to Zach.

***

I stopped at Miss Quetzel's desk before we went outside for recess.

"I need to tell you something," I said, "about Independent Reader."

Miss Quetzel stopped stacking papers and looked up at me.

I took a deep breath and met her gaze. "You know how I was on the top of the list for a while?"

Miss Quetzel nodded. "You've been working really hard on your reading. I'm proud of you, Pansy. It doesn't matter if Daniel has moved ahead in the scores."

I shook my head, "No, that's not what I'm talking about. I-I—the reason I was ahead for a while, is because, um," I cleared my throat, "because I sort of cheated a little." Miss Quetzel's eyes widened. Then she looked toward the front of the room where everyone waited to go outside.

"Class, you may leave and stop in front of Mr. Shannon's class. Please follow his class outside."

We waited for everyone to exit the room, then Miss Quetzel looked back over at me. "Now. You were saying . . ."

"That I cheated. At the beginning of the year, I took a test on a three-point book that I finished right before school started even though we were only supposed to take tests on books we'd read this school year. And then I read a bunch of easy books quickly so I could rack up points. I knew Daniel Walker would be impossible to beat. And . . . and I really wanted to win the trophy this year, that's all."

I dropped my head, unable to look at Miss Quetzel. I knew I'd disappointed her, and I'd disappointed myself, too.

There was silence for a moment. Then I felt a hand on my shoulder.

"It's okay, Pansy," Miss Quetzel said softly. "I know what it feels like to want to win."

I looked up at her, swallowing back tears. "You do?"

"Sure. When I was in school, I was hopelessly average in everything. I was okay in sports, okay in music, okay in art . . . and I had to work extra hard in all my subjects. I was never first place in anything! So, when I became a teacher, I wanted to make sure to celebrate all the little victories. That's why I wanted to give out Reading Bucks to everyone, instead of rewarding only the top readers. When I was in fifth grade, only the A/B honor roll students earned a special field trip, and I made a C in math."

"You did?" I couldn't believe it. My amazing teacher had struggled with math when she was a kid, just like me!

"That's right. And I'll never forget what it felt like to miss out on the trip to the roller rink. So, I decided when I became a teacher, I'd have a party that everyone could earn. Even those who struggled with times tables," she said with a wink. "Listen, how about we just keep that first reading test a secret between you and me? You did read the book, didn't you?"

"Yeah," I said. "It's the best book I read all summer."

"Well," Miss Quetzel said, picking up her jacket and walking with me out the door, "why don't you keep reading books you enjoy and stop worrying about the points? You think you can do that?"

I nodded.

"And by the way, reading picture books is *not* cheating. So you've got nothing to worry about, okay?"

I nodded again. "Thanks, Miss Quetzel." I ran off to join my friends at recess, feeling like a weight had been lifted from my shoulders. Miss Quetzel didn't know the reason why I needed to win that reading trophy. But she had touched on something else I didn't want to admit: that winning for the first time in my life had made me feel good.

"So, what do you think?" Madison asked when I made it over to the playground. She did a little tap dance, and we stared down at her tie-dyed tennis shoes.

"Cool!" Emma said. "Did you do it yourself?"

"Yup. I bought a tie-dye kit at the craft store, and I used an old pair of shoes so Mom couldn't complain."

"Wow," I said. "They look really great."

"Well, I wanted you to know that I meant it when I said I liked your shoes. Even if you did yours by accident . . . hey!" Madison looked down at my feet. "Why are you wearing matching shoes?"

The girls looked down at my old white tennis shoes, the ones I'd found buried in the back of my closet. Dull and ordinary, just like me.

Madison giggled.

"You're certainly good at *not* following the crowd," Emma said. "What happened to your shoes?"

I shrugged. "I changed my mind, I guess."

"I don't blame you," Madison said. "I get tired of doing the same thing all the time, too."

I tugged on a strand of hair. It was way more complicated than that.

But Madison was smiling at me, and I realized that the shoes didn't matter after all.

"Come on," she said, grabbing my arm as we walked toward the playground, the December wind feeling a little warmer than it had minutes before.

## CHAPTER TWENTY-SEVEN

# December 15

Mrs. Liddell called our house the night before the Good Citizens party to say that Andy was going to stay at home. It was the perfect excuse I was looking for. "Since Andy's not going to the Good Citizens party tomorrow," I told my parents at supper, "I'm staying home, too."

Mom looked up from her tuna casserole. "But you've been looking forward to the party for months!"

"It's certainly understandable if Andy wants to stay home," Dad said, "but you shouldn't let that stop you from going."

"I can't go to the party," I said, wishing I hadn't brought up Andy. "I'm still too sore to wear ice skates."

Mom put her fork down. "Is your ankle still hurting you? Because if it is, we need to take you back to Doctor Viera so he can take another look."

"It's not still hurting me. But you need to have very strong ankles for ice skates. Anyway, I just wanted to let you know that I'm not going so you don't need to wake me up in the morning."

I nibbled at my casserole, but I could see my parents asking each other questions with their eyes. They were very good at silent communication because next thing I knew, Mom said, "Your dad and I think it would be good for you to go to your class party, even if you don't skate."

"Who goes to a skating party and sits on a bench the whole time? No," I shook my head, "I told you I'm not going. It's not like I'll be missing any schoolwork or anything."

Of course, my parents tried to convince me. They talked about all the fun I'd have watching my classmates skate and that I'd still get to have hot chocolate and popcorn, and that whenever people came off the ice to rest, I could talk to them. They said it was important to be a part of the group. And, finally, they said that they really wanted me to go.

"It's just a dumb skating party," I said as I helped clear the dishes. "And there's nothing you can to do to make me change my mind."

After I'd finished cleaning up, I went to my room and closed the door. I knew my parents were talking about me in their hushed, worried voices. They wanted Extraordinary Pansy back, but she was gone for good.

I climbed into bed with a non–Independent Reader book that Andy loaned me at the beginning of the year. I was going to stay up late reading and sleep until noon the next day. But something kept tugging at the edge of my mind, and before I could turn the first page, I knew what I had to do.

A box of photos—my Anna box—sat in my dresser drawer. I grabbed my gardening spade, gloves, and a flashlight. After pulling out the box, I threw on a jacket and tiptoed down the stairs. I paused at the bottom and took a look around. Mom and Dad were watching TV in the den, so they wouldn't hear me when I quietly opened the back door.

I closed it slowly behind me and stepped out into the yard. It was a clear night, the stars brightening the dark sky. I circled the yard with my flashlight, stopping when the light landed on the magnolia tree.

Our magnolia tree.

Anna and I had spent hours up in the thick branches, sheltered by a heavy blanket of leaves. It was the best tree for spying. Talking. Giggling. Reading. Observing. It was our own private place, just for the two of us.

It was the perfect place to bury the box.

Keeping the flashlight low on the ground, I followed the familiar path to the tree. I sat down underneath, feeling the cold dirt in my hands as I began to dig. I made a nice round hole, deep enough for the box's final resting place.

I flashed the light on the box cover one last time as I placed it gently inside the hole. The glittery letters danced in front of my eyes. ANNA.

*Don't stop to look,* I told myself. *You've waited long enough. If you want to move forward, it's time to stop looking back.*

But I had to look, just one last time. Slipping my finger under the lid, I lifted it off.

*Just one photo, and that's it. Close your eyes and pick.*

And I did. I turned my flashlight onto a summer picture. The two of us sat on a picnic bench, Anna in a sundress with a matching hat, me in a pair of old shorts and a T-shirt. We held up big slices of watermelon, and we both had big grins on our faces.

*Drop the photo. Stop thinking about it!*

I tried to fight it, but my eyelids closed, and I was pulled into the photo. It was no longer a cold winter night, and I was not in the middle of the yard burying a box of photos.

A warm breeze blew back my hair, and the sun beat down on my shoulders. Anna and I were in the middle of a watermelon seed–spitting contest.

"Your turn," I said with a giggle. Anna held up a big slab of watermelon, took a bite, closed her eyes, and spit. The seed landed about a caterpillar's length away. Sticky juice dribbled down her chin and dripped onto her white sundress. She opened her eyes and burst out laughing.

"I'm up!" I said. "Let me show you how it's done." I puffed out my chest and wiggled my eyebrows. Then I took a bite, sucked off the fruit, pulled in my lips like I was about to whistle . . . and that seed flew across the yard.

"Woo hoo!" Anna yelled. She jumped up and down, pumping her arms in the air. "You did it! That was the best one yet!" And then she ran over and threw her arms around me.

I froze that moment, just standing there, feeling her hug and listening to her excited voice next to me, cheering me on.

Anna was always really good at that.

When I learned to swim, Anna clapped and hooted. It didn't matter that she could already swim laps around the pool. And when I learned how to ride a bike without training wheels, she ran along beside me, even though she learned how to ride two years before. Even better, whenever we played together, she was always telling me that I had terrific ideas. "How do you come up with this stuff?" she'd say. "It'll be *awesome*!"

I opened my eyes, suddenly aware of the photo in my hands. I stared at it a minute longer, then placed it carefully back inside the box.

The watermelon seed–spitting Anna wasn't with me anymore, but I had this photo to prove she existed. And I had memories in my head that I could call up and re-play any time I wanted. And as I thought about Anna and the watermelon seeds, I remembered something important about her. She had taught me all about giving it your best shot. Her seeds landed only a few inches away, but that never stopped her from trying.

And even her sickness never stopped her from trying.

Anna's brain didn't work the way it used to, and she was lying in bed trying to recover from surgery, but every day she showed me what it meant to be tough. A fighter. She learned to walk and even run when doctors said she'd never be able to again. She got in that swimming pool, stuck her head under the water, and kicked with everything she had . . . even if she had to wear a life vest to keep from sinking. She fought infection after infection and made it through surgery that could have killed her.

The last time we spoke was during a fight. But because of Anna, in fifth grade I did things I'd never tried before. Even though I was scared, even though things were tough, I had tried my best. And I hadn't given up.

Until now.

Anna's voice filled my head. *It doesn't have to be perfect, you know. You just have to do it on your own.*

Maybe I wasn't such a failure after all.

I'd finally cut off my hair to give to Locks of Love, even though I ended up with a lopsided haircut and mismatched shoes. I hadn't become number one in Independent Reader, but I'd been top of the list for a while. I wasn't fast enough to win a class race, but I'd learned to skate without falling down. I'd joined Girl Scouts when I wasn't usually a joiner, and I'd learned how to bake cookies because of it. I'd finally stood up to Zach Turansky, and maybe it would stop him from making fun of someone else.

And I'd gotten out there and made new friends . . . even though I thought I didn't want them.

I put the lid back on the box.

Anna was still my cheerleader.

Mom had said that Anna would want me to make new friends. As I scraped the pile of dirt back into the hole and flattened it with my shovel, I knew what she said was true.

Tomorrow morning I would go to the Good Citizens party. I just had one stop to make along the way.

I snapped off the flashlight. Then I walked back across the grass with the box in my arms, holding Anna close to my heart.

## CHAPTER TWENTY-EIGHT

# December 16

When I woke up the next morning, the sun was streaming through my blinds. The house was quiet. Too quiet. None of the usual back and forth chatter between my parents. No clanking of forks against plates or teakettle whistling. Through squinted eyes, I tried to make out the numbers on my alarm clock. 8:27. I tossed back my blankets and raced down the stairs.

"Mom!" I yelled as I found her at the computer. "Do you know what time it is?"

"It's almost eight thirty." My mom looked at me. "I thought you wanted to sleep late this morning."

"I did. But I changed my mind. Can you take me to the skating rink? They're leaving school at 9:00, but we can meet them at the Ice Palace instead."

A smile spread across my mom's face as she popped up from her chair. "Of course I can take you, Pansy. Now what would you like for breakfast?"

"I'll eat anything," I said as I ran back up the stairs for the first time in weeks. "I'm starving!"

\*\*\*

As soon as I was dressed, I walked over to Andy's. I didn't know what he'd say when he saw me, but I couldn't go to the party without talking to him first.

I knocked on the door, my regular knock. *KNOCK KNOCK knock tap.*

"Hi, Pansy," Mrs. Liddell greeted me as she opened the door. She didn't look surprised to see me, which meant only one thing: Mom had phoned to warn them I was coming. "Andy'll be down in a minute."

"Can I see Anna first?" I asked her. "I haven't talked to her since she got back from the hospital."

Mrs. Liddell smiled. "Of course. She's still weak from her surgery," she said as I followed her down the hall. "But yesterday she wanted to get out of her wheelchair, so I helped her take a walk around the house."

"Really? That's great." I peeked my head into Anna's room where she was lying in her bed, watching TV. I blinked when I saw the rainbow-colored hat, remembering that her head had been shaved a few weeks ago. She looked paler and thinner than she had before.

But when she glanced over at me, there was a sparkle in her eyes, like she knew exactly who I was. One side of her mouth turned up in a smile. A real smile, just for me.

"Hi, Anna." I sat on the chair next to her and reached for her hand. "I'm glad you're home."

\*\*\*

"Mom told me you were here," Andy said a few minutes later. I'd been sitting with Anna, filling her in on everything that had happened since she went to the hospital. I looked over at Andy, who stood leaning against the doorway, his hands in his pockets.

"I'll talk to you later, okay?" I said to Anna. Then I followed Andy out into the hall. We stopped in the entranceway. I turned to face him. "Your mom says you're not coming to the Good Citizens party."

"Yeah." Andy shrugged. "I'm not crazy about ice-skating."

"Me neither. But we've worked hard all these past months. It's going to be a lot of fun."

Andy kicked the carpet with his foot. "I'm not really up for a party."

I paused. Then I pulled my hands out of my pockets. "I wasn't in the mood either. I was planning on staying home, just like you."

Andy looked up at me. "Why'd you change your mind?"

I took a deep breath. "Because Anna wouldn't have wanted me to miss it."

Andy didn't say anything. He looked away from me, then he said, "You want to go in the backyard?"

"Sure," I said. We went out the back door, and I followed him up the ladder to the tree house. It had been a while since I'd hung out with him there. I was happy to see that everything was still the same. A couple of beanbag chairs lay scattered across the floor. Shelves were covered with piles of comic books and notebooks and LEGO, and a couple of crumpled snack bags littered the rickety table.

"When Daniel comes over, do you come up here?" I asked him.

"Sometimes. Mostly, though, I like to hang out here by myself."

Last time I'd been up here, autumn leaves had fluttered around us. Now bare tree limbs waved in the December wind. Andy turned and leaned against the large window. I stood next to him, and we both stared out at the tree branches for a long time.

"I'm sorry we've been fighting," I finally said.

"Me too." Andy turned from the window and picked up some LEGO bricks from the bookshelf.

"I shouldn't have said that Anna was a better athlete than you—I was just so angry at you for embarrassing me in front of everyone. You *promised* not to tell anyone about what happened at the park that day."

Andy shrugged. "I guess . . . I'm not sure exactly why I said it. It's just . . . you've been acting so different this year."

I raised an eyebrow at him.

"I mean, what's been with you the last few months? If you hate skating so much, why have you been doing all that practicing? And why'd you spend all that time reading boring books when you could have been doing something more fun?"

"You mean like building Zeraclop City with you? Is that why you started working on it with Daniel? Because you were mad at me for being busy all the time?"

Andy snapped some LEGOs together. "Something like that."

"But I already told you, remember? I was doing it for Anna."

He gave me a strange look, like he didn't remember the conversation at all. "Anna?"

"Yeah. I kept hoping the surgery would cure her, and when she woke up I needed to be the kind of friend she always wanted me to be. The kind of friend who wouldn't let her down. I guess that sounds stupid, to think the surgery would change her back—"

"No," Andy said softly. "It doesn't sound stupid at all."

I looked into his eyes, and that's when I knew. I saw the same deep clouds in his eyes that I saw that day in Anna's hospital room. Andy had been hoping for a miracle, too.

"Is that why you never talked about it?" I asked him. "You didn't want to jinx it?"

Andy shrugged. "I didn't know what was going to happen. It could have been really good . . . or it could have been really bad."

I nodded. "Mom tried to tell me about the risks. But I didn't want to think about it."

"Yeah."

There was silence for a moment. Finally, Andy said, "But I still don't get it. Why would you want to change? Anna liked you just the way you are."

"She used to. But then we got in that big fight before she got sick. You know, about sleep-away camp."

"Oh yeah . . ." From the look in Andy's eyes, I could see he'd suddenly remembered.

"I was trying to make it up to her. I needed to be the kind of person who didn't chicken out of things, someone who kept her promises."

"But what does sleep-away camp have to do with skating? Or Independent Reader?"

"I told Anna we'd take lessons together last year, but I quit after the first time."

Andy shrugged. "Anna got over that pretty quickly. She loved to skate, and you hated it."

"Still, it was a broken promise, just like backing out of sleep-away camp. That's why I joined Girl Scouts, you know. So I'd be ready to go on a camping trip next time she asked. And I cut my hair," I said, running my hand over my hair, which now reached my shoulders, "because I promised we'd do it together."

Andy nodded, like he was finally starting to put the pieces together. Then he wrinkled up his eyebrows. "Still, what does Independent Reader have to do with any of that? Why were you reading books you didn't even like?"

I thought about it for a minute. Being top in Independent Reader wasn't a broken promise I'd made to Anna. It didn't really have anything to do with Anna at all. Had I really been doing it just for myself? "I—I thought I could do it, that's all. Anna would have liked that I was trying so hard and that I didn't quit."

"I guess." Andy paused then shook his head, looking totally confused again. "But—but the whole thing doesn't make any sense! If you were doing it because you wanted Anna to forgive you, then you were wasting your time. She wasn't mad at you anymore. She would have come home, and things would have been just like they always had."

"What are you talking about? If she forgave me, I'll never know it."

Andy shook his head. "No, she really did forgive you. Don't you remember the letter?"

My heart skipped a beat. "What letter?"

"You know, the one she wrote from camp."

"Andy!" I faced him, my hands on my hips. "You never said anything about a letter."

"Yes, I did. She asked me for your address because she forgot to bring it with her."

"She never wrote to me from camp."

"Well, she got sick. Like, the day after I got her letter. I guess she never had a chance to write to you."

I couldn't believe it. Andy had forgotten to tell me that Anna had forgiven me? Was it really true, or was he getting the facts mixed up?

"You never told me about any letter," I said again.

"Come on," he said, motioning to me. "I'll show it to you."

I followed him down the ladder and raced up the stairs of his house. I'd been wondering all this time . . . and there'd been a *letter*? He opened his desk drawer and dug around for a few minutes. Finally, he pulled out an envelope and handed it to me.

For a moment, I just stared at the envelope. I stared at Anna's neat rounded letters, the funny face she'd drawn on a balloon, the address written in purple and green.

"Go ahead," Andy said. "Read it."

I pulled out the letter and began to read, hearing Anna's voice in my head.

*Dear Andy,*

*This camp is AWESOME. It really is! We've done all kinds of exciting things. We hiked through this cave and our feet got all wet and we got completely covered in mud. We swim in the lake with little fish every day. We've gone canoeing (two people fell out, but not me!) and we even went rock climbing. But the best thing we've done so far is tubing on the river. It's so fun and waaay better than going on the log ride at Carowinds!*

*The food is even pretty good for camp food. We have stuff like pizza and baked ziti. And we have desserts like cake and pie and watermelon every single night.*

*If you finished the second book in the Dark and Spooky Castle series, DON'T tell me what happened! I just finished the first book and I can't wait to read the next one when I get back. So, if you haven't finished it, you better hurry up and read.*

*Pansy should have come with me. Because we would have had a blast together!*

*Gotta go help in the kitchen. I have cooking duty tonight, and we're making apple pie.*

*Your amazing twin, Anna*

*P.S. I forgot Pansy's address. So if you see her, will you tell her we're still best friends 4ever?*

I read the letter all the way through, twice. Then I looked up at Andy.

"I thought you knew," Andy said. "I mean, did you really think she'd stay mad at you?"

I felt a smile tugging on the corners of my mouth. Anna wouldn't have been surprised that Andy forgot to tell me, so I knew I couldn't be, either.

"You can keep it if you want," he said.

I shook my head and looked down at Anna's words. "It's your letter, Andy."

"That's okay. I don't really keep stuff, you know, the way girls do."

This time my face broke out in a great big smile. "Thanks," I said, hugging the envelope to my chest. "I guess I'll keep it. Payback, since you never gave me her message."

Andy shrugged. "I'd forgotten all about the fight. I figured you had, too."

I rolled my eyes. *Boys.* No sense getting mad at Andy for thinking like a boy. Then I remembered the skating party. "Hey, I'm just going to run home, and then Mom's going to take me to the rink. We can pick you up on the way, if you want."

Andy pushed up his glasses, shifting from one foot to the other. "Like you said, I'm not much of a skater."

"I didn't mean it! I was just getting back at you because you told everyone that dogs almost pulled me into the duck pond."

"Tiko, Bonsai, and Moochers." Andy grinned. "Remember?"

"How could I forget?" I giggled. "So, are you coming or not?"

Andy hesitated a minute. Then he said, "Guess I better go get my gloves."

"Great. And Andy? I won't tease you about not being coordinated if you promise not to tease me."

"It's a deal."

## CHAPTER TWENTY-NINE

# December 16

It was almost ten o'clock when we pulled up in front of the rink. I spotted the Carvin County School bus in the parking lot and knew that my class was already inside. Pancakes flipped inside my stomach as I thought about tying up my skates and stepping onto the ice.

"Do you want me to come in with you?" Mom asked. "I can help you with your skates."

I shook my head. "Mom, I've done it loads of times. I take lessons, remember?"

Mom smiled. "Okay. Do you have your gloves? Warm socks? Jacket?"

I held them up.

"Well, have a great time!" Mom leaned over and kissed my cheek. "I'm so glad you decided to go."

"Thanks, Mrs. Smith," Andy said as he got out of the car.

"Be there in a minute," I said to Andy. He shut the door, and I watched him walk up to the entrance. Then I reached into my pocket. I pulled out my Best Friends necklace and dropped it into Mom's hand.

"It's broken," I told her. "Do you think you can fix it?"

Mom looked down at the necklace, then closed her hand tight. "Pansy," she said, looking back up at me, "this is one necklace I will find a way to fix."

I gave her a quick wave and got out of the car. A blast of cold air greeted me when I pushed open the doors to the rink. I joined Andy at the counter, and we both picked up our skates and walked over to a bench to put them on.

As we were lacing our skates, I looked up to see the last person I wanted to see tying his boots.

"Your friends were wondering where you were," Zach said to us both.

"Really?" I asked. "Who?"

"You know, Madison, Emma, Daniel, Hannah."

"Oh." I waited for Zach to say something rude. Instead, he finished tightening his skates and gave us a little wave before he took off across the rink.

You could almost call it a *friendly* wave.

Andy and I exchanged looks. Had speaking up to him really worked? Was he going to stop being mean to me and Andy from now on? Had Zach really changed?

Andy stood up on wobbly feet. "Ready?" he said, holding out a hand to me.

I stopped thinking about Zach, focusing on what I had to do next. I pulled the top lace and it snapped off in my fingers. I groaned. "I'm going to have to get another pair. See you on the ice, okay?"

Andy nodded and made his way to the entrance while I took off my skates and returned them to the counter. A few minutes later, my next pair laced, I got to my feet.

It was now or never. I walked to the entrance to the rink and stepped onto the ice unsteadily. Immediately, I hugged the rail.

What happened to all of those weeks of lessons? My ankles felt wobbly after being off the ice for a while, and it felt a lot like starting from scratch.

Was I completely nuts? I should have stuck to my instincts. I never liked skating to begin with, and here I was, in front of my whole class, attempting to ice-skate when I'd just recovered from an ankle injury.

Suddenly, I heard a voice in my mind. *Come on, Pansy!* My eyes snapped shut. I saw Anna's sparkling eyes, her face lit up in a smile. *You can do it!* I took one hand off the rail, and I felt Anna's hand in mine.

I stood up taller, held my head up high, and steadied myself on my skates. I bent my knees and held one arm out, the way Trina had taught me. Then I opened my eyes and glanced down. No Anna beside me—only the cool air brushing against my cheeks. I blinked, the air stinging my eyes.

"Pansy!" I heard my name again. "Hey, Pansy!"

I looked across the rink and saw my friends—Madison, Emma, Daniel. Even Hannah was hanging against the edge. Andy had made his way over and was pulling himself along the rail. Madison waved both arms above her head. Her feet slipped out from beneath her, one, then the other, and she landed smack on her butt. Madison broke into a giggle, and everyone laughed along with her.

A grin tugged at the corners of my mouth.

*You can do it, Pansy.* A whisper, and this time it was my own voice I heard. "You can do it."

It was time to try out my own legs, no matter how shaky they were. I waved back at my friends. Then I let go, gliding on a single blade across the solid ice.

# Acknowledgments

Without the help and support of many people, *Extraordinary* would still be one of the manuscripts filed away in a folder on my computer, simply titled *Pansy*.

It has taken over ten years for *Extraordinary* to take shape and become the book it is today. Thanks to all of the wonderful people who have helped me get from idea-in-my-head to book-on-the-shelf:

My fantastic editor, Julie Matysik, for falling in love with Pansy. Your expertise has made me dig deeper and pushed me in new directions as I journeyed on the path toward publication.

Mandy Hubbard, for your support and advice through this incredibly long process! Your professional feedback helped transform the book into what it is today. Thanks for believing in me and *Extraordinary*, I feel lucky to have had the opportunity to work with you.

My fabulous critique partners: Karen Bly, Eileen Feldsott, Marilou Reeder, and Yolanda Ridge. Your constructive criticism helped me grow in countless ways as a writer, and your hugs and positive words kept me going during the lowest points on this roller coaster ride.

Thanks to Carol Baldwin, for being one of my very first readers of multiple manuscripts and for cheering me on for years and years. A special thanks to Stephanie Gorin, who read and reread *Extraordinary* and continued to offer suggestions and advice and encouragement. XOXO!

All of the other critique partners from the Blue Boards who offered feedback for various versions of the book that eventually became *Extraordinary*.

My mom, for filling the house with books and introducing me to a world of literature.

My dad, for inspiring me with your perseverance and for making me feel like an author at a very young age by making copies of all my "books."

My sister, Naomi Moore, for being my first cheerleader and reading all my early attempts at young adult novels, even those that ended up in the trash can after one hundred pages.

My sister-in-law, Hope Franklin, and my niece, Anna, for teaching me the true meaning of Extraordinary.

My in-laws, Tom and Margaret Franklin, for celebrating everyone's accomplishments, including mine.

My best friend, Liz Neron, for always being there for me.

My amazing daughters, Eliana and Carissa. You are my Joy. I love you up to the stars and moon and clouds . . . and all the way back.

My husband, Scott, for all your support and encouragement through twenty years of marriage . . . and twenty years of rejections! Thank you for celebrating the tiny victories along the way, for printing out the sparkly notes from an agent or editor and hanging them on your office wall, for putting up with me on those days when the news was not what I'd hoped for. *Extraordinary* would not be here without you. I love you, always and forever.

And to my students, past and present, for inspiring me with your perseverance, for making me smile on even the most difficult days, and for teaching me more than you will ever know.